WAR EFFECTS

OBI NNANNA NWABUGWU

War Effects
Copyright © 2023 by Obi Nnanna Nwabugwu

ISBN
978-1-961601-29-1 (Paperback)
978-1-961601-30-7 (eBook)
978-1-961601-28-4 (Hardcover)

Dedication

In loving memory of my late sister, Chinyere Nneka Mbulo – an extraordinary writer who encouraged and nurtured rough writing skills in me. Also, to the evergreen memory of my childhood friend, late Okechukwu Onyegbadue that told me I will someday write a book. So sad they are not here today to read my book.

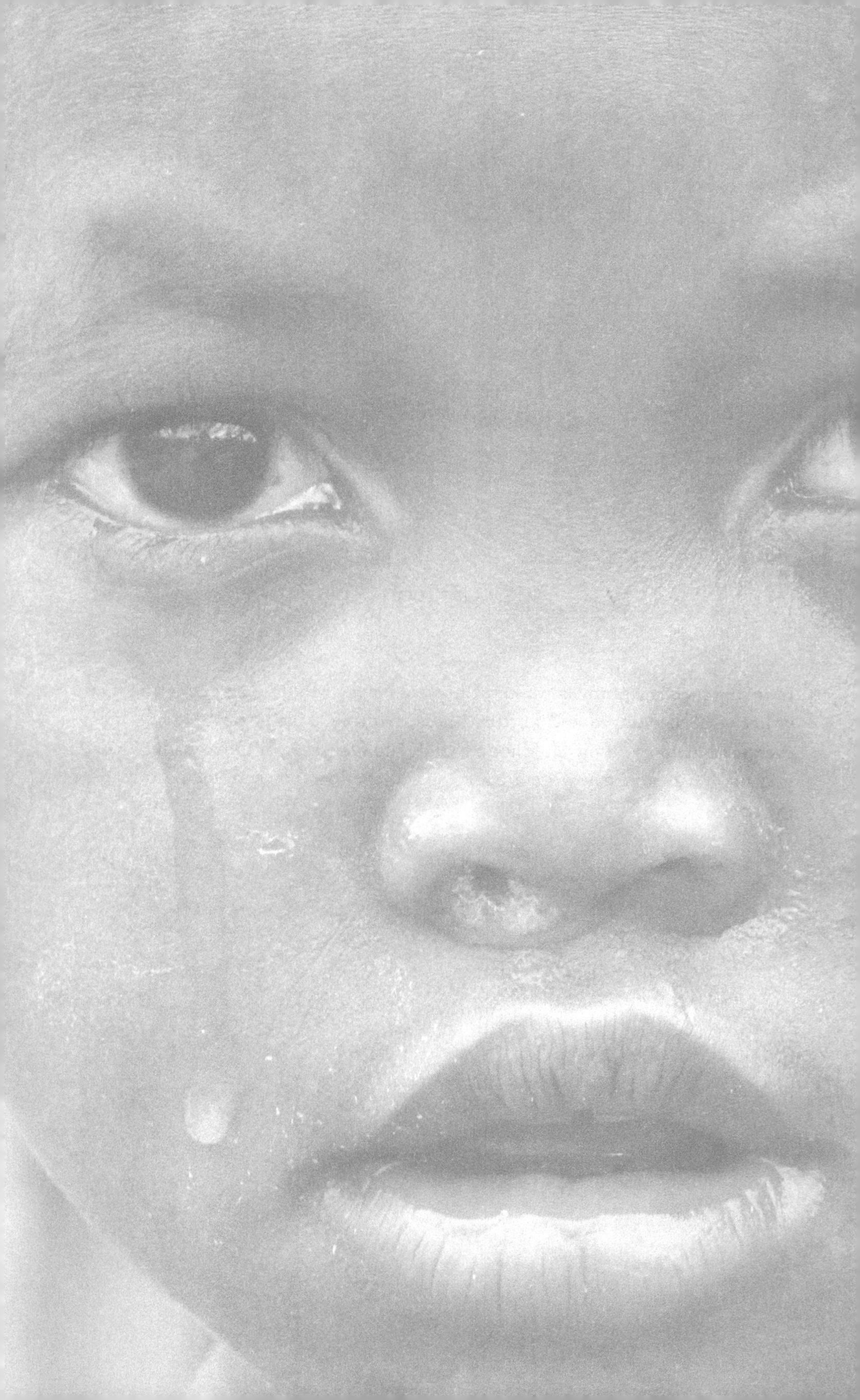

TABLE OF CONTENTS

ACKNOWLEDGEMENTS

My immense thanks go to my dear wife, Dr. Nkechi Nwabugwu; my father, Chief Sir Joel Nwabugwu; my sisters, Uzoamaka and Nkemjika; my mentors – Eze Mbulo, Justus Uhah, Nnanna Okorie, Ben and Pat Onyeise. My special thanks go to the Ihomba Age Grade – Fechi, Tonna, Chidiebube, Chineme, Kingsley Ohaegbulam, Felix Etunwaoke, Esther Ejelonu, Okwukwe Davis Ihentuge and Chukwuma Ofoegbu – who were responsible for the successful completion of this project. My special thanks also go to Joseph Nwogu and Dr. Ruth Oji who edited this book with so much love.

FOREWORD

The book "War Effects" derives from a concern with the contemporary situation in Nigeria in particular and the world at large. It delves deeply into the past otherwise it will be practically difficult to comprehend how the present state of affairs came into being and what the trends are to the near future. From time immemorial, inability to learn from past experience has always been a recipe to decay. Inept leadership by people of unbrokered frame of mind garnished with corrupt mentality has held the country on the jugular. This has made it difficult for her to rise above her teething problems many years after independence. The book shows vividly that the country is treading on the same path that led to the civil war the effects which are still suffered by the defeated - Igbos as war captives. The war led to serious erosion of moral and ethical values and institutionalized poverty among the Igbos which had a spillover effect on the country as a whole. Get rich quick syndrome, such as armed robbery, kidnapping, prostitution, ritual killing for money making and more become a way of life in a country sufficiently endowed with human and material resources. The book emphasized that the scars of war will disappear on the face of the defeated when genuine reconciliation based on full integration of the defeated into scheme of things in Nigeria. Chuks Aashif Haifa who out of desperation to survive strayed from the religious upright way of live which Rev. Father Albert impacted on him. Chuks became a fifth columnist to the course of his people traumatized by war and abandoned by the Nigerian government. Strong moral rectitude, devoid of essentialities of descent living amount to effort in futility

The book is lucidly written in simple and easily understandable form. I therefore applaud the author for this scintillating, informative and unique style of writing. Unique in the sense that a lot has been written on the civil war in Nigeria, however, none linked terrorism in the country presently to the aftermath of war. This is a superlative blend of fiction with reality. Reading the book will revolutionalize a new dawn in book writing especially among young formative minds. This book is thus recommended for widest readership possible.

Nwogu Nkemakolam Nwogu
PhD Candidate University of Ibadan, Nigeria

PROLOGUE

A foremost Political Party in Nigeria requires for immediate collection of forms for the House of Representatives and Senate election primaries, qualified rogues with the following professional qualifications: a first degree in looting, drug pushing, bank fraud and advanced fee fraud; compulsory experience as a state governor that used self-allocated security votes fund to loot his state dry; a professional advanced diploma in aggressive cover-up techniques, both physically and financially, is a plus; foreign account ownership of looted funds in Europe, America, Asia and Cayman Island; must be a duly certified Liar with vast experience in corrupt practices which include ritual killings, assassination of political opponents and government enemies; must be ready to shun the voices of the People in allegiance to the Party's wishes; possession of a falsified educational degree especially from untraceable countries would be an added advantage. Duly qualified candidates should please forward their detailed Resume to the Party Secretariat. Please note that candidates with links to political thugs, militant groups and suicide bombers will be given a preference. The selection process will definitely be biased and open to changes without notice, as this is part of the party policy. Short listed candidates would be given a course in Political Illusion to familiarize them with how to use confusing language for the masses and in the parliament. Marriage of underage girls (from 14 and below) is welcome. This advert did not go down well with Chuks Haifa as he read the article with a frown on his face. He knew quite well that it was referring to him as a Nigerian Senator and his other colleagues in the House of Representatives.

In Paris, a man was shouting angrily in front of the mosque. His face was cold-blooded and his mouth widened like that of an angry lion. "Get that satanic book and burn him with it," said Khameni, to the surprise of the onlookers. After about 20 minutes, he zoomed off in his limousine and started making plans for one of his deadly actions which are always well executed with the intent to leave an enemy napping like a smelly dog.

THE
WAR

LASG
RRS

ONE

"The Scars of war are seen on the children of the defeated" "I am Chukwuma Okoro. Some of you call me Senator Chuks Haifa. I am good looking, 5 feet 9 inches tall and 190 pounds in weight," he boasted. "I have done a lot for this constituency; there is no need to reel off everything I have done. I will do more if you allow me to represent you again in the Senate. Nzo ukwum na eso ihe Zik na Ojukwu chere ndigbo," he said, meaning that his actions will always follow the pattern of what Zik and Ojukwu wanted for the Ibo people. "Nwoke mara nma," meaning "handsome man," someone shouted from the crowd. "Onye oshi," meaning "thief," another person shouted back. "Unu nile no na Senate bu ndi oshi. Kedu ihe unu megoro anyi?" that is, "All of you in the Senate are thieves. What have you done for us?" Another person shouted, "Ofo nfoju akpa ndi senator, Chineke ga akwu unu ugwo ojo," meaning "Senators that only care about their personal pockets, God will pay them back in a miserable way." He ignored the distractions and continued his political lies, with hopes that his thugs would deal with those trouble makers.

Chuks Aashif Haifa was born in Ajegunle, Lagos State, Nigeria, a notorious suburb occupied mostly by low income people. His father was a cobbler and his mother, a cleaner. He was the only surviving child of his parents; the others died before they reached the age of three. His survival was miraculous because everybody thought he would have gone the way of his other siblings. He was born in Adepoju maternity; his mother was assisted by Madam Kofo, the owner of the maternity who was actually a quack nurse but claimed she was trained by the British in Burma. Chuks' parents lived in a one-room apartment in a twenty-room compound with only one toilet facility that was shared by everybody. The toilet was always littered with feces by Ekaette and her children. For them, feces meant nothing bad because it is said that in their village in Annang, people sleep and dine in situations worse than this particular toilet.

Ekaette was a divorcee who engaged in prostitution to take care of her well-fed and healthy looking children. She looked scary because of the kind of hairstyle she always put on. She was very rude, troublesome and lacked respect for her neighbors. Consequently, one of her neighbors, Baba Ijebu, took her for a witch. Baba Ijebu had two wives and eight children who all lived in a one-room apartment. It surprised me how all of them managed in one room apartment. I was told that he used African magic to control his family, but later in life, I understood that it was his wisdom and diplomacy that enabled him to effectively control his large family in that one-room apartment. His first wife, Mama Ijebu, was known as *Madam nothing concern fish with raincoat*. That was her popular phrase each time she talked about her two political heroes, Awolowo and Tafawa. From then on, people started calling her *Madam nothing concern fish with raincoat*. We lived in a big, dirty compound that harbored people with the same dream of finding a better life in Lagos. I used to think that the building would collapse as it used to drip water all over, even when there was no rain. The major thing was that we all came from different tribes to seek a better life in Lagos, but we had one thing in common — we were all poor illiterates.

In the compound everybody respected Mr. Akin, the caretaker. He came from the same village as the landlord. For this, the Landlord made him the caretaker of the compound. He never paid any house rent because of his job as the caretaker. He loved fish and *ewa* so much that Endurance, Madam Ekaette's son, told us that someday Mr. Akin would develop fish fever and die. The notion about Mr. Akin having fish fever and his head turning to a fish head changed when my father told me that Mr. Akin was instructed by a herbalist to quit eating meat, and from then on, he developed likeness for fish.

In our compound lived Adodo Ibrahim, the dirtiest man I had ever come across because he looked like a night soil man. I was afraid to enter his room because of the kind of dirty clothes he wore. I got the shock of my life the day my father told me that Adodo Ibrahim, notwithstanding his dirty nature, had a wife in Zungeru, Niger. I thought no woman would marry him because of his dirtiness. My Mama use to call him *"escape hunter"* because he was very indomitable in arguments. He was well informed, but spoke funny English because he was imitating Mr. Bob, the British whom he served. At times he held on to some funny and stupid ideas such as the white man's feces being bigger and having different colors from those of Africans. Although he said these stupid things, it was through his life experience that I learnt that life was like a cycle and that a man's fortunes could change overnight. This statement was fulfilled in Adodo's life when Mr. Bob rented a better house for him, and also promised to take him to London whenever he was leaving Lagos. The funny thing was that Adodo never wore the good clothes Mr. Bob gave him. Instead, he preferred to wear his old dirty clothes. When Adodo left the compound, we felt his absence. We missed his stories about Niamey, the *Tonyo* city where children rode on goat backs, adults on horses, and how cows sang. We dreamt of going there to witness these wonders, to the extent that I kept disturbing my mother to take me there.

After Adodo left our compound, his apartment was vacant for a long time until Mr. Akin and my Mama cleaned the place and a new tenant moved in. His name was Dagogo, aged about 30 years or thereabout. He had a radio set. In fact, that was my first time of ever touching one with my bare hands – when I lent a helping hand as his things were moved in – and it was a thrilling experience for me. Dagogo was a native of Ogoni in Eastern Nigeria. He told me we were all Easterners and he had a good relationship with my parents. Everybody in the compound liked him except Baba Ijebu. The reason for Baba Ijebu's hatred for Dagogo was that all the women in our compound liked him. Baba Ijebu became jealous of him to the extent of accusing him of sleeping with his younger wife, Oluremi. They all used to say that he had been to England, that is the white man's land but he never told me about the white man nor did I care to ask him about it. He used to tell me stories about his place and the big river he always swims in. He said the river was bigger than Ajegunle and even bigger than Lagos. He was always talking about the frog that swam across the' river Niger and entered the ocean. At times he would buy bean cakes for me, but never for the Annang woman's children. He said they were "Mmuo Otu Okpa" meaning "the one legged ghost."

In the face of such dangerous accusation, my father and Mr. Akin warned Dagogo to be very careful of Baba Ijebu's family. Dagogo, rather than heed to the candid advice given to him, bragged, "I am an Ogoni man, nothing will happen." One day, Dagogo saw fifteen giant rats in his room at a time. He screamed and ran outside. Surprisingly, he saw Baba Ijebu laughing. He told Dagogo, "go back to your room and check if the rats are still there." When he got back to his room, there were no rats to be found! He was confused because he was sure the rats did not leave the room from the front door. Dagogo told some people what happened but no one took it serious. The women in the compound made fun of him. The only people that believed Dagogo's story were my father and Mr. Akin because they knew that Baba Ijebu was a fetish man. Dagogo learnt a lesson of his life from that event because after that day, he was not seen with Oluremi anymore.

One day, Dagogo called me and showed me gold. That was the first time I saw such precious metal. However, it meant nothing to me. He said the white man discovered black gold in his place, Oloibiri. The black gold killed all the fishes in the river and people ran away from the place because they could not drink water from their rivers again. Their farmlands were also covered by the black gold left by the white man. He further related that the white men that came with the company called Shell caused all the problems and disappeared.

On a sunny afternoon in January 1966, my parents and other tenants came back from their workplaces in a hurry. It was unusual, but I was not bothered because we were on holidays then. They were all afraid because a coup had taken place and many people were killed. I recall that my friend once told me that no human being can kill Zik, Awo and Tafawa, except the river mermaid because she had the keys to their lives. I wondered how they were killed in the coup if truly they were above human destruction. I heard them saying that there was also a riot in Kano because Abubakar, Okpara, Sardauna of Sokoto and others had been killed. I was fond of Awolowo because my teacher in the school said he gave children hope by providing free and compulsory education for them. For this particular reason, I cried for Awolowo. It surprised my parents why I liked Awolowo that much.

Throughout that day, my father was disturbed because of his younger brother in Kano. He wanted to send him a telex, but he could not leave the compound because of the soldiers on the streets. The soldiers were whipping people badly and nobody dared venture outside the streets. Everybody was afraid, and it was really terrible within that period. The coup of January, 1966 was one of the major events that changed my formative life.

TWO

After the coup, a lot of things changed in the country; also did the people in our compound. They stopped being friendly to each other especially when the rumors of war started making the rounds. It was as if the war already started in our compound because people from every part of the country lived there. Everyone was so cold to each other. I was very eager for the war to commence after hearing how interesting a war movie could be. Tunde, my friend in school, told me he went to watch a war movie with his father at the cinema. Tunde was a small hero among his peers in school because of the biscuits he often came to school with. He was always telling us stories about war movies. Life began to change and all of a sudden everybody started planning to go back to their villages. Before I knew what was happening, Papa had already booked a place in a truck for me and Mama. I was warned not to tell anybody that we were going to the village because of the war. Papa said that war was a terrible thing, but he supported this one coming up because many people of the Igbos were killed in Kano riots. My father was visibly worried because he had not heard any news about his brother in Kano and as such, he was not sure if he was dead or alive. The telex he sent had not been returned.

Lagos was not what it used to be anymore; the whole placed changed overnight. Edwin, Papa's friend came to our house in the evening to warn Papa to quickly move to the village as fast as he could because, according to him, "levels dey rough now, make you see say wahala dey Lagos ooh. I have already sent my family to the village and will be leaving by next week," he told my Father. He mentioned that he got authentic information from Hausa traders from Kaduna who sold goats to him, that Ojukwu had taken control of Eastern Nigeria and that soon the Federal government would declare war on Biafra.

Due to so much pressure and fear, Mama became sick again, behaving abnormally. She charged at Baba Ijebu and chased all the children in the compound away with a broomstick. However, Dagogo held her and calmed her down. The disgrace was too much for Papa when he came and heard the story. There was nothing he could do but to call a herbalist after apologizing to Baba Ijebu. The herbalist gave mama a black liquid inside a dirty bottle to drink. The portion calmed her a bit, but Papa said that the best thing to do was to send her to the village as soon as possible. We were not the only people leaving for village from our compound; Dagogo was traveling too. He had secretly made an arrangement and had packed all his valuables inside his tin box.

Two days later our traveling arrangement changed because Papa decided to go with us to the village. Dagogo too would join us in the new truck booked by Papa. The plan was that when we stop at Owerri, Dagogo would continue his journey to Port Harcourt. Papa packed my clothes in a plastic bag and other valuables inside our box. I was so excited I did not know when I told Effiong, the Calabar woman's son about the planned trip. When I realized what I had done, it dawned on me that if Papa found out, he would whip me mercilessly.

Apart from that, I was filled with so much excitement because Dagogo told me that in the village, one could climb trees, go to the river to swim and do fishing. He said that there were many nice boys and girls to play with. He also said that the bushes in the villages were very large and had elephants, birds and all kinds of animals. I asked Papa about these things and he confirmed that they were all available. Papa told me that in the village I could go for bush-rat hunting just like every other kid in the village. The best of all the news for me was that there were varieties of food in abundance, in the village. He said that I could go to the farm, pluck or dig up any type of food I wanted.

Village sounded very interesting to me, but Mama's sickness and the upcoming war overshadowed the excited feelings I had had. On the day before we left for the village, the herbalist came to the house, lit a candle and applied a concoction of oil and repugnant smelling leaves on Mama's forehead. The concoction made Mama sleep off after complaining of dizziness.

Before the herbalist left, he gave Papa another bottle of the mixture for safe keeping until she would have need for it again. This time the bottle was clean, with a plastic cover, unlike the previous one which was covered with leaves. However, he told Papa that before we boarded the truck, he should give her a bit of the portion. When we were leaving the compound, it was a shock to Mr. Akin as he took the keys to the rooms from Papa and Dagogo. This development caused a big quarrel between Dagogo and Mr. Akin, as both shouted at each other. Everybody in the compound came out watched what was going on.

After much argument, they agreed that the keys would be with Mr. Akin, but he would be responsible for any loss of items in the rooms and was never to rent it out to another person. To get to the motor park, Papa hired two wheelbarrows pushed by two dirty young men wearing only singlet. One of them said, "Omo Ibo don dey travel finish." Papa looked at him and laughed. Dagogo was behind us following the wheelbarrow man carrying his luggage. Not long afterward, we arrived at the motor park. That was the first time I entered a truck, although Baba Rere had driven me and Effiong in his Morris Minor. This time, I did not have to wash my legs before entering the truck. Baba Rere would never allow any kid to enter his car without inspecting his feet and clothes.

The truck was big and dusty with broken wooden chairs. We were all jam-packed on the wooden chairs and underneath them were our boxes. When the conductor was inspecting the truck, he was angry with the amount of load it was made to bear. He brought down the dog, goat and pounding mortars that a passenger brought along with her, claiming that the animals were looking sickly and the other luggage, smelly. When the passenger insisted on traveling with them, the conductor threatened replacing her with another passenger. The chaos attracted the attention of the driver who cautioned his conductor and begged the passenger to keep calm. But in the end, the dog, the goat and the cooking mortars were all rejected. The passenger that owned them had to be replaced by another passenger.

By 10.30am, everybody was seated on the truck. I sat on my own unlike other kids who were carried by their parents. Some people stood at the back of the truck. I heard Dagogo call them 'attach'. Stingy people that can never pay the full fare price for such a long trip. Before we left, Papa bought a plate of rice with an egg. Surprisingly, he gave me the egg, which on a normal day, he would never have allowed me eat it because according to him, egg makes children steal. The bus conductor gauged the tires before the commencement of the journey. He initially used his legs to kick on the tires before adding more air to it. He also poured water and oil into the engines. A woman prayed as we were about to move. However, her prayer took so much time to the extent that the driver got angry and started the truck engine and that stopped the prayer. I wondered what kind of prayer that was. When we eventually moved, I was happily seated between Mama and Papa, with Dagogo at the end of the chair.

Mama drank the herb and slept off immediately. The journey was difficult for me because I sat down for a very long time. The roads were very dusty and the truck stopped several times on the way. To make the matter worse for me, I contended with a full bladder several times during the journey. My father had to call the attention of the driver to stop so that I could ease myself. Unfortunately for me the driver said that he would only stop at the next junction thirty minutes away. He said that he was afraid we might be attacked by armed robbers if we stopped indiscriminately on the way. Somehow, I held on till we reached Onitsha junction before I could urinate. Papa told me that that was Zik's State. It was as dirty as Ajegunle city, with lots of tall buildings scattered everywhere. Everybody seemed to be in a hurry, and the streets were lined up with small shops where all kinds of things were sold.

As we stopped, the conductor woke up from his sleep and went to buy kai-kai, a local gin made from ethanol. When he came back, the woman that prayed before the commencement of the journey shouted at him, saying "be careful with the way you consume kai-kai in this truck because kai-kai is the devil's drink." The whole thing was funny to Dagogo who winked at me after the admonition. We arrived at Owerri the next day. The truck stopped at the motor park and the prayer woman shouted, "Praise the lord!" "Alleluia" my Papa and others responded happily.

THREE

Dagogo left us at Owerri amidst tears, hugged my Mama and told her, "doo". That was the last time I saw Dagogo in my life, I was later told he joined the army and died in Benin. I still remember him till date because he was really a nice and friendly guy. Papa hired another wheelbarrow that carried our load to the Mbaise Park, a small park with only three trucks. Owerri was a smaller town compared to Onitsha. Most of the people there were neatly dressed and carried themselves with an air of pride. Papa told me that Owerri is a civil servant town. At the Mbaise Park, the bus conductor that assisted us was by my estimation a few years older than I was. I was surprised to see young people of my age grade doing the bus conductor job. So was my mother who had woken up from her sleep. She uttered "tufiakwa," meaning "God forbid," to show her displeasure.

We waited at Mbaise Park for more than five hours before the truck moved and it was getting late by then. When the truck started moving, the little bus conductor hanged on the truck. The people at the park called him actor which he relished while winking his eyes at the people each time they called him the name. Mama was really scared of what the bus conductor was doing. "This small boy go soon die ooh," Mama exclaimed. This attracted the attention of the driver who stopped the truck and ordered the conductor into the truck. When the little boy came into the truck, he murmured, "This Lagos people again with their wahala." Papa overheard him and threatened slapping the hell out of him. To my surprise, the little boy replied, "Nothing dey happen." Mama calmed Papa down. "Leave this little devil alone," she said.

On the way to Mbaise, we passed a lot of small houses with trees and flowers beautifully adorning them. "Wow! Mbaise is really a village!" I said to myself. It wasn't long before we arrived at the park in Mbaise village. The gate was manned by a horrible looking old man that had a bad dentition. As soon as he saw Papa, he said, "Nwa town." Papa replied, "Dee James" he hugged him. Before we knew what was happening, many people came and assisted us with carrying our luggage to the house. This was a true manifestation of the village spirit that Dagogo told me about. People were nice to one another, unlike in Lagos where such kind of a thing never happens. Nobody cared about the others but in the village everybody cared about one another.

As soon as the women saw Papa they shouted in ecstasy and danced around the house. They carried me shoulder high; making me feel very special, something that I had never experienced in my life. Dagogo was a prophet because everything he told me started to be made manifest the same day of our arrival to the village. No wonder he said that the village was better than Lagos. The roads in the village were not big enough for the vehicles to pass because they were too close to the houses. The village was quite interesting because everywhere was in the state of nature with sweet smelling aroma from the surrounding bushes. Many people in the village looked dry and worn-out because it was the onset of the farming season. People leave for their farms as early as 5 am in the morning only to come back in the evening. This had great strain on their health. In the village, children of my age move about unmolested – something quite strange to me. In Ajegunle, children cannot move about freely on their own for fear of being kidnapped or run down by moving vehicles. I was a superstar among the children in the village because I came from Ajegunle, the Ghetto City of Lagos. They flocked around, touching the cloth I wore, but the women shouted at them to leave me alone. I never realized how important I was to these children until I interacted with most of them.

When we reached Grandpa's house, the women gathered, singing praises to God for our safe arrival. To my surprise, Mama comported herself well because she did not put up any impression that suggested that she was sick. They women admired her plaited hair and clothes she was wearing. However, I could not understand what was fantastic in her clothes which were no better than what poor Oluremi in our compound in Ajegunle usually wore.

Grandpa was a wealthy man based on the economic indicators for measuring affluence in the village. He had a magnificent house built from a mixture of red mud and cement, 15 goats, 20 fowls and many plots of land. On our arrival he instructed that a chicken be killed and used to prepare special soup for us. Grandpa told me to join the fowl chase with the children around. It was indeed a thrilling experience chasing after those fast running chickens in the compound. We caught the biggest fowl among those we chased, Grandpa was so happy that he called me "Agunna". The children around all burst into laughter and started calling me Agunna which eventually took over my real name.

"Seat beside me," said Grandpa. I obliged. However, I was disgusted at his body odor caused by constant sniffing and licking of tobacco. Grandpa gave me a big chunk of the fowl meat including the head because I was the first male child of my father. Grandpa ate in a very funny way; his fufu balls were so large that I wondered how he was swallowing them. Everybody seemed to keep quiet whenever he was speaking. People respected him a lot in the village and he would never tolerate challenges from the way he looked around when he talked. He presided over all village functions including conflict resolutions and traditional marriage ceremonies. Whenever a cow or goat was slaughtered in the village, a better part of the meat was reserved for him. The next day, Papa took me and Mama to visit our relatives. He said it was the tradition. People in the village did not know me and mama. We received warm greetings wherever we visited and they were all friendly and dirty. The older men also had brown teeth like grandpa. I later found out that tobacco use was the cause of the dirty, bad dentition among many of them in the village. I was given plenty of bush meat and groundnut. Everybody seemed to like me. I really felt like a superstar those early days in the village. I suppose it was a kid's way of thinking that gave me the perception that the village was all good no matter what.

Following the breakdown of the peace accord between Col. Ojukwu and Gowon in Aburi, Ghana, many people came home to the village. The war was not important to me. The only thing I cared about was going hunting for bush rats and picking snails in the bush. Whatever the elders were saying about the war was none of my business. Papa always went to Dee Willie's house to listen to and translate whatever was said on the radio in English to the villagers concerning the ongoing war. Papa was among the few people who could read, write and speak English by the village standard. I was sure Papa was not that good in English but the poor villagers had no choice than to believe whatever he told them. Grandpa used to tell me that I must go to school to be wise like the white man. "My son will school in Government College, Umuahia and will bring the white man to this village," said Grandpa. Each time Grandpa mentioned the name of Government College Umuahia, I got flattered because it was not easy getting admission into the school. Because I could recite ABCD to Z very well, Grandpa was confident that my intelligence would afford me an admission into Government College, Umuahia.

FOUR

We got news from a man that just returned from Kano that my father's only brother had been slaughtered in Kano by the Hausas during the riots against southerners. The news was first relayed to the village Head, as was the tradition. He was scared of delivering it directly to Grandpa because he was afraid the old man would collapse on hearing the death of his second son. The village Head summoned the elders and deliberated on how to break the news to Grandpa. The news spread quickly in the village without any member of my family hearing of it. That evening all the elders came to see Grandpa. They chased away all the women and children around. The village Head cleared his voice and said, "Nwoke oma", meaning "Good man, we have come to deliver a message which only the gods can bring and only real men will hear and stand their ground." Grandpa had the feeling that something had happened. "Did I commit an abomination in the land that has warranted the visit of the elders to me at this time of the day?" Grandpa sniffed a big chunk of tobacco, adjusted his shoulders, wiped his face and sat calmly like a brave man as he waited to hear from the elders.

"The village Head said that information reaching us from Kano is that your son is dead and his body cannot be brought back because nobody knows where he was buried," an elder managed to speak. Immediately the elder finished, Grandpa stood up and sat down. When he stood up the second time and was about to fall on the chair, the elders rushed at him, grabbed him in his confused state and told him to be a man. "The life of a great and illustrious son of this village has been cut short by barbarians in the North Grandpa said". Hold your father, the elders told my Father. Wailing and crying pervaded the village immediately the news was broken to our family members. Grandpa, in grief, said that he regretted allowing him to go and live in the North.

War was now in full swing. News came in that the Nigerian soldiers had bombed Asaba Town, killing many people, especially women and children. The elders said that not even an ant was left alive by the mean Nigerian soldiers. They said that most of the soldiers were Muslim mercenaries from Niger and Chad. The village Head called a meeting to warn everybody of what would happen to us should the Nigerian soldiers get to Mbaise. Food was scarce and young men were forcefully conscripted into the Biafran army. Grandpa hid me all the time, away from the prying eyes of the Biafran soldiers while Papa always hid at the bank of our village stream, Mmiri Udo River. Grandpa did not want to lose his only surviving son to the war again.

The war brought out the worst of behaviors in our teenagers, a lot of rape cases were perpetrated and disrespect to the elders was at a high level. Most of the elders became agents to Biafran soldiers – passing on information as to where the children of those they disliked were hidden and this caused a lot of problems among families. There was this man from my village, Joel by name and an accountant in a reputable British Motor company in Port Harcourt. At the peak of the war, the white men in the company left the country for their safety, leaving all the cars and other valuable properties of the company in the care of Joel the accountant. Joel took some young men from my village and drove all the cars to Obizi for safe keeping. Twenty big trucks were brought to Obizi. Some days later at night, a group of young men from my village led by Johnny came, stole the trucks and sold them to Nigerian soldiers at Onitsha. The village was taken aback by the sudden disappearance of the trucks without any trace. Grandpa took me to visit Joel's father on the issue. This incident brought shame and disrepute to our village and the neighboring villages ridiculed us as thieves that stole from their brother.

Food became very scarce in the Eastern region because Awolowo whom Ojukwu released from prison in Enugu turned around to work for the Nigerian Government. Grandpa said that Awolowo had the brain of two people combined together and more dangerous than the rattlesnake. It was Awolowo that brought the idea of food embargo on Biafrans, saying that hunger will make them turn against Ojukwu and the war will come to an end. Many children in the village developed kwashiorkor, a disease characterized by protruding stomach caused by protein deficiency. I was fed with lizards and grasshoppers to complement for protein loss because I was looking emaciated and dry. Cassava leaves and other bitter tasting leaves were used to prepare soup for me. Grandpa told me that any child that died from Kwashiorkor disease was thrown into the evil forest so that the disease would not infect others. However, later in life I became aware that Grandpa was wrong about his perception of Kwashiorkor disease because it was not a contagious disease in our biology class in the school.

Constant air, land and sea bombardments in the Biafran territories became daily occurrences by the Nigerian Army. People could not sleep with their two eyes closed. Even at that tender age, I was very scared that we might be killed from the air strikes. I cried to my parents and Grandpa to take me to a place that I will not hear the sound of the air strikes anymore. Hunger became a secondary issue now in my life. My father told his kinsmen that Nigerian troops had advanced to Orlu town in Imo enroute to Ahiara Mbaise where Col. Ojukwu made the famous declaration commencing the war. Everybody needed to get prepared to leave the village immediately to a safer environment. Papa came into the house visible agitated. I asked him what the matter was because he was talking to himself. He told me that the situation had gotten out of hand because the Nigerian soldiers were very close then. "What about the Ogbunigwe bomb discovered by Biafrans," I asked Papa. Papa said America and Britain were fighting on the Nigerian side but Biafrans were on their own, with the exception of Gabon that was helping them by also taking many little children as refugees. Grandpa resisted my going to Gabon with the fear that I might not come back again and that my Mama was too sick to lose her only surviving child.

News came in again that Nigerian forces had entered Mgbidi town, killing everyone in sight when they conquered it. Everybody was afraid that these soldiers would kill us if they got to Mbaise, but Grandpa erased such thought, saying that it will never happen since it did not happen in Onitsha when it fell to Nigerian troops; although it happened in Asaba and Mgbidi. Mama's health condition got worse by the day. This was owing to the war conditions since she could not have access to treatment. She could not eat anymore or talk to anybody. The nearest hospital was controlled by Biafran soldiers for the treatment of their wounded colleagues first before any other person. It was really a tough time for our family because food and water were scarce commodities then. Yam, cocoyam and cassava that were left in the farm had been stolen by the few young men that evaded conscription into the Biafran army. The reality of the war was now telling on everybody. Our village became a ghost town as most of the young men and women had all gone to fight a war with the belief that it was for the survival of the Igbo nation.

Papa told his kinsmen that BBC reported that morning that Nigerian soldiers had captured Port Harcourt and very soon, would take over the whole of southeast Nigeria. However, the war propaganda machine of Biafra led by Okoko Ndem refuted the claim as balderdash and that Biafra was winning the war. They people were confused the more with such information because if this was true why were there no food and water for the people. In my little mind I was beginning to understand what war was all about. Children were prohibited by their parents from playing outside for the fear of kidnappers working for the Biafran soldiers who took little kids as spies and sent the rest to Gabon. Such was the fate of Okey boy who until now is nowhere to be found. Uncertainty, fear and confusion enveloped the entire village. It was chaos all through the village. I became a man overnight, given the daily occurrence of the war as told to me by my Grandpa, my father and witnessed by myself. The tall dreams I had about the village evaporated into thin air because of the war.

FIVE

"With the fall of Port Harcourt, Onitsha and Asaba, it would only be a matter of time before Owerri and Aba would fall into our hands," boasted Nigerian troop commanders Murtala, Obasanjo, Buhari and Adekunle who were advancing from all directions. In the face of the reality on ground that the war was not going as planned, Grandpa was resolutely in support of the cause the Igbos were pursuing, saying, "My son Ojukwu has tried for the Igbos. He used the wealth of his father to fight their cause. I hope he will not be killed, Oh God of Israel. What will happen to us after the war? We will be treated as slaves by the Hausas and Yorubas." His main worry was about the fate of the Igbo children and their future. "Look at how they killed us in a most barbaric manner in Kano; pregnant women had their stomachs slit open. Uwa ahuhu ka umu anyi na aba na ime ya," he lamented. He meant that a life of suffering awaits our children if this war is lost. It was difficult getting food to eat in the village to the extent that lizards, grasshopper and rats had all disappeared. Any family that could muster one square meal a day was regarded as an affluent one. Wherever smoke flames were seen oozing out from a house, people would rush there hoping to find what to eat. Times were very hard, but Radio Biafra war propaganda kept telling us that Biafra was winning, while BBC reported the gains made by the Nigerian Army. Grandpa knew the war was almost lost but he would never admit it to anybody.

At night on the next day, screaming of the villagers pervaded the entire place because there was the rumor that Nigerian Soldiers had entered Mbaise. Papa and Grandpa woke everybody up and instructed that all of us to move towards Umuahia where other people were running to. It was obvious that Mbaise would fall, given the mass exodus of people towards Umuahia. The line of frantic people running away from the war was frightening. Mama became a big burden now to us but Grandpa insisted that she must go with us but if her condition got worse, we would take her to the Red Cross camp once we get to Umuahia. He insisted that she would be better off with the Red Cross care than with the Nigerian soldiers who were known to take women to their camp and do whatever they wanted with them. It was a shame that most of our women defected to the Nigerian camp. They were disgraceful women who sold their dignity for whatever reason. The trek to Umuahia was long and arduous. Mama was carried by Papa and Dee Reginus, stopping at intervals to take a rest. They were encouraged by the huge crowd of people trekking with them to safety from the war.

We reached Umuwawa Bridge at dawn and Grandpa insisted we rested for a while before crossing towards Umuahia. I put my little sack on the floor besides Mama and other family members traveling with us. Grandpa was indeed tired of walking but he boasted that the journey so far was a small distance compared to the long and tedious trekking they embarked on while fighting along with the British in Burma where he saw white men killed like rats. He went further to say that the white captain under whose command he fought gave him a medal for an act of bravery. He gnashed his teeth saying that old age had dealt a blow to him else he would have been fighting alongside Ojukwu his beloved and brilliant officer.

At the break of dawn we saw many people running from the Umuahia side towards where we were. The news was that Aba had fallen to the Federal troops and that they were almost in Umuahia. There was confusion everywhere, but notwithstanding this danger, Grandpa said we should move on to Umuahia so that Mama can be taken to the Red Cross centre. As my whole family was on the long bridge, Nigerian Planes attacked. It all happened so fast and the bridge was bombed. I just did not know what happened afterward. All I could remember was that I was almost crossing the bridge and was pretty sure that all my family was already on the bridge. The next thing I noticed was that I was pushed off to the edge of the bridge with bloody stains on my body. A look inside the Imo River revealed headless piles and mangled bodies of human beings afloat the river. It was a horrific sight and people were running in different directions. The Air raids were coming from different angles and I could see ragged Biafran soldiers running without directions and formations. The Nigerian soldiers were now shelling everywhere. I had to run for my dear life into the bush near the river. The old man that rescued me from the river fled without looking at me. It was all man for his life. When war comes, family is no more family, friends change attitudes and thinking values come with strange psychological behaviors that take over the souls of people. Imagine this man rescuing me from the river but leaving me to flee for his dear life! I ran into the bush and hid under a big, old tree. I lay quietly in the woods, scared of being captured by the Biafran or Nigerian soldiers. The war was bad for young defenseless ones like me. Okey boy's disappearance now came to my mind. I was really hungry to my bones but was scared to come out of my hiding. I was wounded on my buttocks. The shrapnel had pierced my buttocks. It was a sorry site as I could not sit down but I just lay there like my world was over.

SIX

I woke up with a loud shout from the bites of multiple soldier ants that were biting all parts of my body. My sore buttocks area was not left alone too. My shout attracted some ruffling noise that was coming towards me. I tried to be still but the noise was coming closer. I knew they had seen me so I tried to get up and run but my legs gave away and I fell down again. Coupled with the intense pain and my hands scratching away the soldier ants all over me, it was a futile getaway attempt. From a little distance, I could see two men in Army uniform with one of them bearing the tribal marks all over his face like that of Baba Ijebu in Ajegunle. I knew it was the Nigerian Soldiers and I immediately expected some big trouble. But to my utmost surprise they did not shoot me, for they figured out I was an innocent little kid. One of the soldiers looked at my body, with dry cakes of blood all over me and signs of severe hunger plus weakness showing all over me. These, I feel, touched his hard heart to help me. The other soldier was less concerned about me. He had red eyes but was really dark skinned to a fault. The soldier with the tribal marks on his face helped me out of the soldier ants' area, dusted all the ants off my body and carried me on his back. I heard his colleague telling him that I can be a Biafran spy and that he should leave me alone since they could get killed because of me. He ignored him and insisted on taking me along even though

I was an enemy. This singular act from God saved my life. He walked for like 50 minutes and took me to their little camp. I did not know what happened again, the next time I woke up was in the Red Cross hospital in Umuahia. How I reached there I could not tell and it was where my family initially wanted to take my Mama but I eventually ended up there.

The Red Cross center was filled with a lot of injured people, kids with Kwashiorkor and people at the point of death. I was laid on a mat because the beds were not enough. Moreover, bed space preference was given to those with very serious injuries. There were many expatriate doctors, Roman Catholic Priests and Reverend Sisters working there. When the Nigerian soldiers conquered Umuahia, they took control of the Red Cross center. We were taken good care of in the camp with food items such as cornmeal, meat, okporoko, fish, egg, bournvita, biscuits and bread. No more grasshopper and lizard soup. Whenever I was sick, the doctors administered painful injections daily on me to bring life back into me. Though life was better now, I was haunted repeatedly by the thought of my family members and others that lost their lives on the bridge due to the air bombardment by the Nigerian army.

Six months after I came to the Red Cross camp, the war was officially brought to an end due to the surrender of the Biafrans and with Ojukwu fleeing to Ivory Coast. Many of the abandoned children were reunited with their parents, some died of Kwashiorkor and more kids joined us at the Red Cross camp. Father Albert was giving us moral instructions based on bible teachings and life experiences. He told us not to see ourselves as disabled children because there is ability in disability. He urged us not to lose hope in life because of the loss of our parents or loved ones, but rather, to let such experiences be a challenge that would motivate us to succeed in life. He was very impressed with me because I showed much brilliance in the way I correctly answered almost all the questions he asked me. However, the problem I had was that I stammered a lot and that made it difficult for me to express myself fluently. The kids laughed at me each time I answered a question but I would always answer it correctly notwithstanding. Father Albert developed a special interest in me because I was a very smart kid. Most of the priests, sisters and expatriates working at the Red Cross camp attested to this saying that I was a raw talent waiting to explode.

My brilliance attracted many friends to me in the Red Cross camp, among which were Uzo and Ifeanyi, who became my best friends. Ifeanyi was older and bigger in size than I was but he was a talkative. He protected me from other boys trying to bully me because of my outstanding qualities and the attention given to me by the authorities at the center. He had a special likeness for me. Uzo was light in complexion, and probably my age mate and was smart too. Father Albert liked him too and always sent us on errands.

As the Red Cross center was winding up its activities in Umuahia, and with Father Albert moving to head a parish mission in Onitsha, he found himself in a dilemma of either sending us back to our families or taking us along with him to Onitsha. Meanwhile, Ifeanyi was taken to the newly created motherless children's home in Abayi Ngwa. I was not happy with this development but could not help it because it was beyond me.

THE EFFECTS

SEVEN

Father Albert found out that I was from Obizi, Mbaise and Uzo from Umuaka, Nkwerre and decided to drive to Obizi first and then to Umuaka to seek out our families. On Friday morning, Father Albert put me and Uzo at the back of the Red Cross Range Rover, a big pleasure car meant for very important people. We were very excited and felt very important riding in the same car with Father Albert. We sat quietly at the back seat with Sister Juli, the white nurse that treated my wounds and equally developed special likeness for me. I fetched water every day for her before she would wake up in the morning. She sent me on errands and in turn, gave me chocolate. I cherished the sweetness of the chocolate to the extent that I licked all my five fingers clean in an attempt to relish every bit of it.

In our company was Agidi, an ugly man and driver to the Red Cross center. The kids used to laugh at him because his name Agidi is a local Igbo delicacy made from Corn and because of this Ifeanyi boycotted eating Agidi food. The kids never laughed at him in his presence because he would give them hard knocks on head, saying that it was due to their bad behaviors that their parents abandoned them. He would never discipline any kid if sister Juli was around because she would not tolerate any act of aggression and brutality on any of the kids.

The drive was unpleasant because the roads were bumpy due to the effects of the war. People were very careful about traveling around the Eastern part of Nigeria because of the unprecedented high rate of criminality. There were no jobs, only hopeless and homeless people on the street, proliferation of guns and people shooting at each other for minor issues. Civil order had not yet been restored. Soldiers were patrolling everywhere without police presence. As a precautionary measure, Father Albert took his rifle and placed it in front of the car. We could not go through Umuwawa bridge because it was destroyed during the war and was not yet repaired. Instead, Agidi drove through Obowo, a long and horrible road, until we reached Mbaise. Agidi asked questions on the way on how to get to Obizi which was an hour journey from Obowo. I was relieved with great joy and happiness when Agidi said we had reached Obizi.

The whole area had changed dramatically with damaged houses everywhere as evidence of war and destruction. It took a while before Agidi saw a woman that directed us to Grandpa's compound. When she was asked by Agidi about Otawaike, which was Grandpa's nickname and means a man who solves difficult problems, she was unwilling to answer the question as she suspected that the entourage was government agents because of the white people among us. She sighed, and said, "Go there and see things yourself," pointing towards the direction of Grandpa's house and quickly disappeared. Agidi suspected that something was wrong as he drove towards my compound. I could not recognize my house again as wild grasses had overgrown everywhere. I looked around the place I used to play and it looked strange now. Agidi parked, everybody came down and told me to lead the way. I walked towards a woman who recognized me and she started wailing, which attracted many villagers to the scene. Father Albert and Sister Juli wondered why the wailing instead of a happy reunion. The women hugged me with tears in their eyes and men stood in disbelief that I was alive. It all dawned on me that something was very wrong.

Agidi summoned courage and asked what was going on. He was told the plain truth that the whole of my family members perished on the Umuwawa bridge bomb attack by the Nigerian army. Nobody thought I survived. It was really tough for Agidi to relate the news to Father Albert and when he did, it was in broken English, "Father, they say war kill whole family for Umuwawa bridge bombing." Father Albert was stunned by the ugly news and related it to Sister Juli who hugged me like a mum does to a loved child, with tears trickling down her eyes. She kept saying repeatedly, "God will take care of this situation. This happened for a purpose in your life." It was heartbreaking for her, even with all the courage she had exhibited in treating war victims of their wounds and observed little innocent kids die of severe kwashiorkor. This incident was too much for her and she decided taking me and Uzo with them, a decision that changed the course of my destiny for good in life. There was no way she was going to leave me in this place with no family.

She walked up to Father Albert and told him, "We are going with these kids," wiping away the tears in her eyes. She shook her head and told Father Albert, "Nkwerre is cancelled; we head back to Umuahia right now. I will figure out what to do with these kids. In God I trust; they will get the best in life." She said this looking straight into father Albert's eyes. He agreed with sister Juli taking us along. However, Agidi advised that the elders should be told of the white man's plan for little Agunna as I was known in the village. The plan was a welcome development for them because they were only interested in taking over our ancestral family lands should I fail to come back alive as the only surviving male child of my family. My emergence from the blues would have made it tough for any of them to claim our lands. The elders had to let me go with the white man while pretending to be unhappy with the decision of letting me go with the white man. However, some were jealous because they would have loved their children to be with the white man. In all it was one less burden and it did not bother anyone of them at all. They blessed me and let me go with the white missionaries and reminded me to always come back home to propagate my linage, but it was all pretence.

The trip back to Umuahia was an emotional one for me, I cried all the way with Sister Juli cuddling me in her arms like my mother. Uzo urged me to stop crying and face the reality of losing my family members in the attack by the Nigerian army. Losing every member of my family was a traumatic experience in my life which I would not want to happen to any child in life. When we arrived at the Red Cross camp, Father Albert broke the sad news to the community. They commiserated with me and urged me to move on as all will soon be okay because God loves orphans and is always with them. Sister Juli's work was over in Nigeria and she went back to her congregation in Aberdeen, Scotland, for a little break before moving on for another assignment. Father Albert stayed put in Nigeria to rebuild the Eastern part of Nigeria ravaged by civil war and he was made the parish priest in charge of St Jude Catholic Church in Nkpor near Onitsha city. He took me and Uzo along with him and enrolled us in a primary school and we assisted him with the parish work. Agidi did not go with us, rather he was retained as the driver in the Red Cross rehabilitation center in Umuahia, whose head office have been relocated to Port Harcourt city. Agidi told me and Uzo that we were lucky to be chosen among the good boys that passed through the Red Cross. He advised us to be 'good boys and make good use of this opportunity presented to us by the white man,' looking straight at me all the while he was talking. He blessed us before leaving for Port Harcourt.

EIGHT

Father Albert was given a heroic welcome by the people of Nkpor Parish; men, women and children lined up along the road singing and dancing when Agidi dropped us. Father Albert bought a pair of shoes and some new clothes for us. We looked nice and neat, worthy of living with a Reverend Priest of Father Albert's status. The parish was not that small as envisaged by Agidi who left immediately he dropped us at Nkpor Parish house. It was a medium sized church with an assistant priest from Kogi in the Northern Nigeria, who was attached to Father Albert. Father Albert's quarter was a two room apartment with bed and mattress in each of them and had a cook that cooked meals for everybody. He took the spacious master bedroom and put me and Uzo in the other room. Uzo warned me seriously not to bed wet the mattress. The parish church and quarters were cleaned on weekly basis by the parishioners while I and Uzo alone could clean Father Albert's room. Things really moved on fine from that point. We started school at a local primary school down the road with Father Albert taking care of our fees and books. I was so smart that I was moved from Primary one to Primary two after the first term. Uzo was not that lucky but he topped his class in Primary one while I topped my class in Primary two. Father Albert was not surprised by our progress in school and he was very proud of us. We were regular in church activities, page boys in the church and were given the privilege of carrying the Holy Communion during Sunday service. The popularity of the church grew rapidly because it had a white man as its priest who preached in Igbo language once in a while. Father Albert learnt Igbo language fast and communicated with the people in vernacular which made many like him and worship with us in Nkpor. The locals insisted that if a white man can learn their language with ease and in short period of time, why would their children not learn the white man's language? This increased primary school enrollment geometrically during the tenure of Father Albert as the parish priest. Sunday school attendance for kids, population in the parish as well as the revenue of the church doubled in a twinkle of an eye. He was highly commended by the Onitsha Arch-Diocese, the biggest diocese in Southeast Nigeria. To that effect, a certificate of commendation and a brand new Peugeot saloon car were given to him as motivation for hard work. Sister Juli always wrote Father Albert enquiring about our welfare and prayed that God should continue to be with us always. Uzo had not heard anything about his family up until now. His case was worse than mine because there was no clue of what happened to them and by now they would think he died during the war. After about four years it was time for Father Albert to move on to another parish. The Diocese wanted to keep him at Nkpor parish but the Vatican had a bigger role which they thought he was the one fit to handle the job. I was now in Primary six and preparing to take exams into Secondary School. My teachers were pretty sure I would go to Government College, Umuahia or DMGS, Onitsha, the top schools in the Eastern Nigeria at that time.

The Bishop sent for Father Albert because he was needed in Rome by the Pope in two weeks time, it was an urgent message that came out of the blues.

NINE

The orphanage in Aba where Ifeanyi stayed was in a horrible and dilapidated state. The government did not care about the welfare of the orphans there. It was more of a motherless torture home for the kids there because they would go hungry for days without food. Life in the Red Cross camp was far better than the one at the Aba orphanage. The workers were owed months of salary arrears. Individuals who were concerned by their plight donated the little they could to support them. Ifeanyi's main concern now was how to feed; schooling was out of the question. The situation was so bad that the home had to close because the Federal Government took no interest in whatever was happening in Eastern Nigeria. As far as most Nigerians were concerned, those that lost the war were third class citizens. Times were terrible, indeed, for Ifeanyi in the motherless torture house as it was a reflection of how Biafrans were treated in those days. Ifeanyi could not go to school like most of the boys from Biafra. A trader had to adopt him at the Ariara market and he slept in the shop as there was no space in the one room apartment that Dike the shoe trader lived in. Ifeanyi was part of the market vigilante security outfit because his master allowed him to sleep in the shop. Ifeanyi enrolled in the adult education evening classes. They only accepted him because he came from the motherless babies system and the youngest of the people there. The teacher was impressed with Ifeanyi trying to learn how to read and write. He was doing all of this for five years. The tradition of master/servant contractual agreement permitted settlement of the servant after five years. When it was eventually time for Dike to settle Ifeanyi, he told him that he had to serve him for four more years, thereby making it nine years before he could settle him so that the young lad would be able to set up his own little business and grow from there. Dike's excuse was that the business was slow and he cannot settle him from his capital. Ifeanyi had no family to complain to. It was Dike's wife that influenced him to take such decision. Ifeanyi knew that serving his master for four more years would not be possible, so he stole a sack of shoes, took seven thousand naira from their sales and left for Onitsha, first thing the next morning. Dike came in the morning and looked for Ifeanyi but he was nowhere to be found. He went to the bank to see if Ifeanyi paid in the money from the last sales, but he discovered that his account was short of seven thousand naira and that a sack of shoes was missing. He reported to the market vigilante, police and whoever he could tell that the evil boy he picked from the motherless home has killed his business. He did not want to tell his fellow traders how much was missing. Instead he said it was almost all his capital. People that knew how mean he was to Ifeanyi did not feel for him. The market vigilante did not bother to look for Ifeanyi. Instead, they said amongst themselves that Ifeanyi should have taken more from his greedy boss.

TEN

Ifeanyi made his way to Lagos from Onitsha in the morning through "Ekene dili Chukwu" transport service bus. The bus driver helped him find a hotel where he slept for the night. He kept his money in a small jean short inside the trousers he wore. In Lagos, luck was his second name as things moved progressively well for him. Ifeanyi lodged in a cheap roadside hotel in Oshodi occupied by prostitutes who plied their trade, attending to their customers all day long. Ifeanyi got a room on the down floor from where he would head to the Lagos Island shoe market to negotiate and arrange how to sell the shoes he brought from Aba. While eating in the hotel in the morning, he met Teresa a prostitute in the hotel who took him to Lagos Island and helped him sell some of those shoes. It was pretty difficult for him to get a shop because he had little money with him and he could not easily find someone to do business with because he was new in the market. He then bought a wheelbarrow with which he used to sell his shoes on the busy and dangerous Oshodi road. It was really difficult for him to even sell one shoe in a day so he had to change his line of business, with the help of Teresa, to selling pirated music records. His condition got so bad that he moved into Teresa's room but had to hang around the street or go to somewhere else whenever a customer came. He knew what Teresa was doing but he had to survive first. Teresa fell in love with him and helped him with little pocket cash while urging him to get a factory job in the Indian owned metal fabricating company. He was scared of working in such a place after he heard that a lot of people lost their fingers on the machines they worked with and that the Indians were mean and wicked to the Nigerians working with them. For these reasons, he was reluctant to consider that option. It was until Teresa talked to one of her customers Charlie, that things started changing for good for Ifeanyi. Charlie drove fleet of cars, dressed nice and neat all the time. He threw money around whenever he came to the hotel, to the extent that all the prostitutes wanted him like a hot dog but he always came to Teresa. Nobody knew what kind of work he was into but he was stinking rich. A lot of people thought he was into money rituals or doing something bad to live this big. In Nigeria, anyway, whatever you do to make money does not matter; the society does not care as long as you have the money. How you made it does not matter to anyone. Teresa begged Charlie to help Ifeanyi. Charlie did not agree to help at first until he met Ifeanyi and liked his carriage and personality at first sight. He found out that Ifeanyi could write and speak English to a good extent and he figured out that Ifeanyi will be somebody he can use for a while. Charlie took Ifeanyi to his expensively furnished duplex in Ajao Estate. He was not married but lived with three boys working for him. The agreement between Charlie and Ifeanyi was that Ifeanyi will be coming to work from Teresa's room during his apprentice period. Charlie took care of his boys very well and Ifeanyi was a pretty quick learner. The business was to write thousands of scam mails to multiple people telling them different stories about money that needed to be claimed. They got numerous replies from foreigners who needed their help to transfer their money from foreign banks, but in the process, they were scammed.

The boys sourced for fax lines and luckily for Ifeanyi, in his first six months his fax line yielded a job of $200,000 from a man in Singapore. His English was very good and most of all, he was that lucky. Charlie gave him 10% of the money from that deal. When he changed it to naira he was 100,000 naira richer. He nearly went crazy because he could not believe mother luck could smile on him through a prostitute within a short period of time. Teresa was very happy with the sudden development of things around Ifeanyi and she was rewarded with new clothes, shoes and 5,000 naira by Ifeanyi.

Things were so good for Ifeanyi in the first year in the business that he moved Teresa to an apartment. However, Charlie was very angry with the development. Ifeanyi was so smart that the tone of his letters was like that of a lawyer. He developed new formats and methods of scamming people. He introduced Abacha format, NNPC format, lottery format, love format and presidential format. He was so smart that Charlie's big friends wanted to work with him. In the process he got to know a lot of people in that business; even guys in America, Europe and Asia wanted to transact business with him. Ifeanyi was now on his own having completed his apprenticeship with Charlie who now exposed him to the real secrets of the business. He took Ifeanyi to an evil forest in Asaba where he sucked the breast of the mermaid witch called "Nwanyi Asaba." With this ritual performed any person he talked to on the phone will do exactly whatever he was asked to do. "Once a mugu starts to pay, he would continue to pay until he or she dies or commits suicide," said Charlie. It was only the biggest boys in the business that had access to that cult. They performed terrible rituals before they could see "Nwanyi Asaba" to renew the tongue hypnotizing power. Ifeanyi was initially afraid to go, but for anything that would give him money and make him a rich man, he would never slack.

It was a successful trip to Asaba. He sucked the horrible breast of a 100 year old woman. His mouth was cleansed with human blood and he was given twelve chewing sticks soaked with human blood that were left to dry. He was told that whenever he wants to speak to anybody on the phone for business purpose, he should chew the stick before talking. With powers in his possession, coupled with luck and his smartness, a lot of foreigners were scammed. An old man in Australia that he scammed sold all his property including the house he was living in and committed suicide after he lost all that he worked for in his lifetime to Ifeanyi. The lady in America that fell in love with him jumped into River Mississippi and committed suicide after she found out that the person that wanted to marry her and whom she had sent all her savings plus a loan from the bank, was fake. Ifeanyi was now a cultist with no human heart. What he worshipped was money and nothing more. He became a household name and was always seen among very rich and powerful people in Lagos, Nigeria.

ELEVEN

Father Albert came back from Rome and went to the Bishop who was aware of what was going on. His holiness, the Pope, appointed Father Albert to go and establish a church in the Islamic Republic of Sudan. The Islamic Government in Sudan accepted the request for a church in Khartoum and promised not to impose any restrictions that would hinder its smooth operation. There were series of protests because of the presence of the Roman Catholic Church in Khartoum by the different Islamic sects. However, the government stood firm on her decision. Father Albert wanted to go with somebody he trusted and the person that came to his mind was Chuks, because of his loyalty, smartness and dedication to the church which had grown since the time he was in the Red Cross center in Umuahia.

Father Albert decided to keep Uzo in the care of a trusted church member, Anayo Odenigwe, the ex Biafran soldier who lost his left leg in a mine attack. Father Albert met Anayo Odenigwe first in Red Cross camp when he came for treatment at the time when the Red Cross in Aba was controlled by the Biafran Soldiers. His left leg had to be amputated and everybody thought he would die from the wound. When the Nigerian army conquered Aba, Father Albert, Sister Juli and the Doctors at the Red Cross camp ensured that he was not taken away by the Nigerian soldiers. It was a surprise reunion when Anayo

Odenigwe found out that Father Albert was the parish priest in Nkpor and he played an active role in making sure that Father Albert settled comfortably there. How Anayo Odenigwe became very rich in a very short time surprised everybody including Father Albert. People in Nkpor said he used his left leg for money rituals and as such many people avoided having much contact with him. His electronics shop was one of the biggest in Onitsha Main Market. He soon became a household name in Onitsha traders association. Anayo Odenigwe was an illicit drug peddler who shuttled from Hong Kong to London. His involvement in illicit drug business was accidental. In one of his usual business trips to Hong Kong to import radio sets, Mr. Yu, a Chinese radio dealer told Anayo that he will introduce him to a fast moving business that would make him very rich overnight. Anayo Odenigwe was transfixed by what Mr. Yu told him. His thinking was that Mr. Yu wanted to increase the credit facilities given to him by an additional two or three more containers of goods to sell and remit his money to him. However, it was an entirely new business proposition. Mr. Yu took Anayo Odenigwe to a secret chamber in his office and brought out a white powder that he called Cocaine. Anayo Odenigwe asked him what the powder was all about because he knows that Mr. Yu was not was in cosmetic business line. Even if he was, how on earth can it be a powder business? How is he going to make plenty of money with powder that is sold as little as 50 kobo a bottle in Onitsha Main Market? Mr. Yu must be a big joker, he thought in his mind, but he remained calm and waited to hear what Mr. Yu had to say.

Mr. Yu told Anayo, "This powder will make you very rich, only if you can conceal a sizeable quantity of it inside the prosthesis on your amputated left leg and hand it over to my contacts in London. The more of this substance you deliver, the more money you will be paid. A trip of delivery will fetch you $25,000 on a flat rate." He stared at Mr. Yu in disbelief, with his mouth wide open. Imagine me making $25,000 in one business trip when compared to the meager $6000 he makes from selling a container load of electronic set. "Whoa," he said, "what is in this cocaine that makes it so expensive in London? Is it only in London that it is so expensive?" he asked. Mr. Yu then sat him down and properly briefed him what cocaine was all about and the imminent risk involved in the trade – life jail if caught with it. But Anayo Odenigwe was not deterred by this threat saying, "Bullshit, how can they catch Nwafor Nkpor? Agam agacha ije anua nata na udo," he boasted in Igbo language, meaning nobody will catch him, for he would embark on this journey and come back in peace. Mr. Yu assured him that his guys will take care of his passage in Hong Kong airport but he has to take care of himself at the London airport and that he will commence in four days if he agrees to the terms and conditions of the business trip. He immediately told Mr. Yu that he is very interested and even joked about it that if he is in London Jail he would be fed like a white man. Mr. Yu and associates coached Anayo on how to act and to identify the receiver that will pick him up at the London airport. Mr. Yu told him that if he successfully delivers the goods, he should leave London that same day to Liverpool where he will take a connecting flight back to Nigeria and not Hong Kong. He was never to remove the Leg prosthesis on any condition until the package was delivered. The receiver would give him prosthesis of the same size and everything else in the taxi. They would not board him on disabled airline help, but once the plane lands in London, he would tell the air hostess that he is disabled and that he needs airline help on a wheel chair. That way he would not be properly checked by immigration at the point of entry into London. Mr. Yu told him that he trusted him to deliver the job because he will be a least suspected person at the airport because of his disability and that Africans are not known for drug business at that time. The British know that the Chinese own the business right now and will never suspect an African, so Anayo is the perfect match at this time. Anayo Odenigwe's prosthesis was taken by Mr. Yu and a large quantity of cocaine was stuffed in it after which it was sealed professionally like a manufactured product. He practiced walking with it because it was heavier than it used to be and it made his movements slower. A day to the trip, he fasted and prayed his rosary asking for God's guidance on the business that just came to him from nowhere. His ticket, passport and Visa were crossed checked by Mr. Yu before he was driven to the airport. His passage at the terminal in Hong Kong was smooth, the immigration officer on duty made sure he was not checked before he boarded the plane. The long direct flight was smooth and once they landed in London he requested for airline assistance due to his disability. The air hostess had a lot of pity for him and made sure he got a wheelchair and airline helper. He was barely checked at the point of entry because of his condition. In fact, his passport was just stamped and the custom officer waved him into UK with a warm and welcoming smile.

The receiver was already in the airport lobby looking around frantically and ready to take off in case things had gone wrong. But to his joy and relief came Anayo Odenigwe being wheeled out by an airline staff. The Chinese taxi driver was already outside waiting and picked them up immediately. Right inside the taxi, Anayo Odenigwe's prosthesis was switched and he was dropped off at the bus station with an already paid ticket to Liverpool. He was relieved and thanked God for blessing him. News reached Hong Kong that the package was delivered intact. Mr. Yu and his associates celebrated a mission well accomplished. Anayo Odenigwe left for Nigeria the next day from Liverpool and Mr. Yu called him 6 days later in Nigeria telling him to come back to Hong Kong two weeks later for his share.

That was how Anayo Odenigwe got into drug peddling business. He went a couple of times before he retired and invested his money in his transport business. He bought six 50 seater luxurious buses for a mass transit company that he opened. He donated substantially to the purchase of a brand new Peugeot 504 car for Father Albert by the Nkpor Parish. He is a man of action when it comes to money issues in Nkpor. Before Father Albert left for Sudan, Uzo moved in with Anayo Odenigwe. He was in Primary five and surprising passed the entrance to DMGS Grammar School. Anayo Odenigwe held him in high esteem because of his intelligence. He called him "Nwa Father onye ocha" meaning the son of the white priest. This brought him closer to Anayo Odenigwe who consulted him in his letters and proper record keeping of his money. Uzo was enrolled in DMGS but Anayo Odenigwe wanted him to join his business when he finished secondary school. After five years, Uzo graduated from Secondary school and joined

Anayo Odenigwe in his business. Anayo Odenigwe had increased his fleet of cars. Therefore, he trained Uzo to take care of the electronic importation business from Hong Kong. Traveling abroad to buy goods was the dream business of every young man in the Eastern part of Nigeria, including Uzo. Uzo made several trips to Hong Kong which gave him the opportunity to know Mr. Yu better.

Notwithstanding the death sentence imposed on drug trafficking in Hong Kong and many parts of Asia, Mr. Yu continued with the business. Rather than become deterred, he even became more sophisticated in the business by increasing his cocaine courier contacts and transportation to London in Nigeria, Ghana and Equatorial Guinea. He introduced Uzo into the business by linking him with some Chinese businessmen in Lagos, Nigeria. In Lagos, Uzo swallowed some wrapped quantities of cocaine and dropped them in London before transiting to Hong Kong.

The actual preparation and packaging of the hard drug are done in a hotel in Lagos with the help of an unnamed Chinese contact person. The cocaine was wrapped with water in latex condoms or rubber balls as they call it. He swallowed 100 wrapped balls of cocaine with milk and was told not to eat or drink fluid until he reaches London in order to avoid bursting of the stuff in his stomach or increase the urge for bowel movement. He was also given an acid reducer and bowel movement inhibitors medications before and after swallowing the drugs. "Good luck with your Easter eggs," said the Chinese man who did not tell Uzo his name or leave his contacts. Cocaine trafficking carries a big risk of death should it burst in the stomach or jail terms should the person be caught alive. But for the huge return in investment, Uzo was convinced that the money was worth the ultimate risks involved and was hardened with this notion at the back of his mind.

Anayo Odenigwe unaware of Uzo's foray into the illicit drug business started seeing big changes in the way Uzo spent money and thought that he was stealing his money. To this effect, he instructed the manager of one of the First bank branches in Onitsha where Uzo had an account to tell him secretly how much Uzo had in his account. The bank manager initially did not agree to do so because it is unethical. However, when Anayo Odenigwe threatened to withdraw his money from First Bank, the fear that losing such a customer will attract a memo from the headquarters to him since the account was so loaded, made him succumb. The only condition was that Anayo Odenigwe should never disclose to Uzo how he found out his bank details. The bank manager disclosed that Uzo had nearly 2 million naira in his account. "Chei nwa egbuo mu o," he shouted, meaning 'this boy has killed me.' He went to his shop in the Main Market. In anger, he slapped Uzo and told him to walk out of his office. Uzo was surprised and confused with this sudden development. He asked Anayo Odenigwe in a subtle, low tone what the matter was. People gathered around and tried to calm Anayo Odenigwe down, but all to no avail as he shouted the more, "I picked this boy from the gutter and this is how he is repaying me by stealing my money and lodging it in the bank. Do you know who I am? Even with one leg, I will deal with you very well," he threatened Uzo. "You are out of here and that is final." People were surprised at what was going on, considering how close both of them were. Tears now filled down Uzo's eyes, he could not believe this was happening to him. He knelt down crying and begging his master to let him explain himself. "It is all over, you have to go. As long as I, Anayo Odenigwe is alive, Uzo, you are ex-communicated from my life.

Uzo left that night and stayed with one of his friends in Onitsha for a couple of days while sending people to beg Anayo Odenigwe, but all to no avail. Uzo did not want to explain to anybody how he got the money, fearing the backlash he would get from people that he was involved in drug peddling. God forbid! "Nwa Father," how would he face the people and how will Father Albert take the news that Uzo is a cocaine trafficker? He maintained his innocence that he did not take a penny from Anayo Odenigwe, saying to him, "Go to the bank and have them print your statement of account so that you can know whether any money is missing from it. Surely, I will not give you my money even if the heavens come down," Uzo said.

Uzo left for Lagos and established a small scale electronics business in Ladipo market with the help of a business associate that Mr. Yu introduced him to. He called Mr. Yu and told him everything that transpired between him and Anayo Odenigwe. Mr. Yu told him that he is welcome to Hong Kong anytime and that he will sell goods to him on credit. Uzo rented a small apartment in Lagos and continued the cocaine business with Mr. Yu and other contacts he made in Lagos. He made a lot of money from drug business and instantly became a Big Boy in Lagos. Coincidentally, he met Ifeanyi in a mega club in Lagos. They exclaimed and exchanged pleasantries, phone contacts, visited each other often, chased women together and became good friends again. It was indeed a great re-union for both of them. This time, though, they were in a different world of young rich men.

TWELVE

Father Albert came back from Rome after meeting with the Pope. He had only two months to move to Sudan. He informed Chuks that they would be will be traveling together to Sudan. The news of Father Albert's transfer to Sudan was received with shock in the Nkpor parish. It did not go down well with them. As a result of the impending journey, Uzo, Anayo Odenigwe and Chuks all came together again after a long while. Uzo was not happy with Chuks because he was always favored in everything by Father Albert. However, he could not complain to anybody but took it as the wish of God, as Father Albert had taught them to abide by it. Chuks and Father Albert traveled to Enugu where they were given international passports. At the Sudanese Embassy Chuks and Father Albert were given multiple years' visa with resident permit. "Sudan here I come," Chuks said to himself, because he was very excited about the journey. Following this, he went to his class teacher and asked him where Sudan is located in the world scene. His teacher showed him the world map which confirmed that Sudan is in Africa. Father Albert was blessed and offered lots of gift items by the congregation, but he rejected them saying, "Give them to the destitute among you, I do not need them". He bought new clothes for Chuks before the departure. On the day of their departure, Uzo was in tears because he was going to feel greatly, the absence of Chuks and Father

Albert. The ride from the East to Lagos was exciting. Chuks had never traveled on a chilly air conditioned luxurious bus before. He wrapped himself in the arms of Father Albert because of the cold air from the air conditioners. The Nigerian Airways plane that took them to Sudan worsened the situation for him because it was cold throughout the journey. Fortunately, he was given a blanket by the cabin crew to cover himself. They were served a variety of food and drinks and that made the journey a pleasant one for Chuks. "Plane is good ooh!" he thought in his mind. He was excited by the forward and backward movement of his seat each time he pressed the button on the handle that he kept pressing the button until the man sitting at his back patted him on the head to stop. Father Albert cautioned him to behave himself and he did so throughout the journey.

The airport in Khartoum was more beautiful and neat than the one in Lagos; Chuks came down from the plane through a self propelled stair that amazed him and prompted him to ask Father Albert the mystery behind the stairs. Father Albert replied that it was a product of 'oyibo wonder'. "This is turning out to be interesting," he said to himself. When he got down the stairs of the plane, almost all the people in the airport were dressed like the Hausas in Nigeria, with long flowing black gowns that covered every part of their bodies, except some parts of their faces. "Who are these masquerades?" he asked Father Albert. They reminded him of Mmanwu Otigba (the flogging masquerade) in Nkpor which comes out during the new yam festival and flogs anybody at sight. Father Albert told him to relax; that they were Muslim women in their traditional attire and they are nice people but he should be careful because men are not permitted to go near them unnecessarily. This was lesson number one in Sudan and also a caveat emptor for him. It is not going to be easy, he thought. When they were cleared by the immigration, a Sudanese Christian officer welcomed them from the airport in a way quite different from that in Nkpor. They were taken straight to a hotel room because the apartment they were to stay in was not ready yet.

The parish in Khartoum was a small one. It was just the opposite of Nkpor parish, with few members. At times there would be only fifteen people in the church service on Sunday. Preaching in the open was forbidden, let alone getting a television slot for airing Christian religious preaching because it was an Islamic state. This notwithstanding, Father Albert kept on reporting to Vatican about the progress he was making. Money realized from the church activities was nothing to write home about. It was not enough to pay for the apartment he lived in. Were it not for the assistance from Rome, Father Albert would not have been able to run the parish. Three years of study at home made life very boring for Chuks. To this end, Father Albert sent Chuks to a higher institution where he earned a diploma degree in Political Science and later proceeded to undertake a Bachelor's degree program at the University of Khartoum. Studying Political Science was a dream coming true for Chuks who was very conversant with current happenings in the world. He was very intelligent to the extent that he passed the entrance to the university.

Sending Chuks to obtain a university education turned out to be a big mistake that Father Albert did in Chuks life. Chuks, being a very smart and politically conscious student, won the admiration of his professors who encouraged him to join the school political club. His popularity spread like wildfire in the campus and attracted much publicity to him. However, being a foreigner as well as a Christian was unfavorable to the majority Muslim population in the school. A Sheik saw him, liked him and tried several times to convert him to Islam. He did not tell Father Albert what was going on because he knew that Father Albert would not want to hear anything like that. Already Father Albert was not happy with his mission in Khartoum because the Muslim dominated population was making it difficult for his church to grow. The parish was subjected to consistent attacks and vandalization by Islamic fanatics. The membership of the church was dwindling daily with constant threat on converts to Islam to face instant death. Chuks was no longer serious with church activities because of school politics and was always in the company of his numerous Muslim friends. These, Father Albert noticed and became more agitated. For Chuks, he knew that Khartoum would be a tough place but it was tougher than what he was experiencing now.

THIRTEEN

Sheik Maliki thought that converting Chuks, an altar boy of the white priest, to Islam, would lead to an elevation of his status and image in Sudan. That would be a victory for Muslims and also make him popular in the Islamic world. "This will open a lot of opportunities for me," he said to himself. Sheik Maliki devised plans to actualize his dream by carrying out a detailed researched of the Ibo race through the Sudan Embassy in Kano. He found out that the best way to get the Ibo man is through materialism. The Ibos love good things of life and have a great love for money; Chuks would be no different.

Sheik Maliki told one of his students, the son of the ruler in Libya, of his plan to convert Chuks to Islam and that he would need his assistance. The student would need to convince his father to help execute the plan. The plan was to include Chuks among the group of Muslim students that would go on all paid two weeks study trip of the political system in Libya, in addition to sight-seeing. Chuks was so excited about the trip, told Father Albert about it and he did not object to it. For Father Albert, he wanted Chuks to go and have some fun after a hectic period in the school.

When they got to Tripoli it was a ravishing beautiful city like those of Europe and America. They were given very important persons' treatment right from the airport. They were ushered into a waiting

Limousine and driven to a five star Sheraton hotel and towers. Chuks and his colleagues were taken aback with the treatment they were given. "Is this really an excursion or something else?" they wondered. Chuks was the only non-Muslim in the group of five selected students. The guide told them that they will meet the ruler's son by 11am the next day and that they should make sure they are ready before 10.30 am. The night was long for Chuks, but by 10.30am he was all dressed, had his breakfast and was ready to go. They all rushed down to the waiting car that drove them to the presidential palace. It was the most beautiful building in the world he had ever seen. They were ushered into one of the smaller guest rooms and to their surprise Sheik Maliki was already seated there. The greeted him and sat down beside him. He told them that he was invited by the ruler's son. They were served a variety of good food and wine beyond what they could consume. The wine, inside exquisitely designed bottles, was refreshingly nourishing. The chairs were made from the cedar wood of Lebanon and coated with gold. The design could be likened to those found inside the biblical Temple of Jerusalem erected by King Solomon of Israel.

They sat down carefully in order not to stain the chairs. However, Sheik Maliki did not talk to anybody again but got busy reading his holy Koran. After about an hour, the ruler's son came in and introduced himself and apologized for coming late. Everybody was impressed by his humility. The palace was manned by fierce combat ready-looking muscular tall guards and soldiers carrying AK 47 riffles. The students were taken around the presidential palace museum to see the political history of Libya. While walking, the ruler's son tapped Chuks on the shoulder and said, "I would like to see you later today. My driver will pick you by 8 pm." Chuks heard the president's son telling Sheik Maliki that he discussed with the ruler about the project and that the ruler had promised to handle the matter by 9 pm today. Others in the group were wondering why Chuks was told to come back. Shema jokingly said that perhaps they want to have rough sex with him because most of these super rich men are homosexuals. Because of this, Chuks wanted to decline the invitation but Shamali insisted that he should go and keep the appointment saying, "Sheik Maliki cannot think evil for you."

As discussed, the chauffeur picked Chuks up by 8pm on the dot and drove straight into the presidential guest house. Acting on instruction from above, an Italian lady walked him straight into the private presidential guest room. There, Sheik Maliki, the President's son and the President were all seated and waiting for me. I was so afraid that I missed my step before taking a seat beside Sheik Maliki. "Come over here my son," said the ruler. "I have heard so much about your intelligence and smartness," said the Libyan leader. "Are you of the Ibo tribe of Nigeria?" he asked. I replied, "Yes, your Excellency." He spoke in a clear Arabic English accent with so much authority emanating from each word that came out of his mouth. I was surprised to see such a ruthless and pompous man talking to a commoner in a humble manner. I sat speechless beside him and paid rapt attention because he was a man that had power of life and death. "Your people lost the war," he noted. "Yes, your Excellency," I acknowledged. "I understand that majority from your tribe are Christians, does that make you a Christian too?" I nodded in the positive. "Do you know that most young men in your country from the Hausa and Yoruba tribes are on government sponsored university education in different parts of the world? Sincerely speaking, there are about 200 Nigerians on government scholarship here in Libya and my advisers told me that none is from the Ibo tribe. Why is that so in your country?" he asked me. Before I could provide an answer to his question, he sprang on his feet and with a voice filled with anger he asked me, "Are the Ibos third class citizens in your country?" "Your Excellency, I am not aware of that," I replied. He continued, "Do you know that in your Federal civil service, a Hausa Diploma holder heads an Igbo man with a Master's degree?" he asked. I sat there perplexed by what he was saying because those were indisputable truths on ground in Nigeria but I wondered how he came about these revelations. "Is it because you people lost the war? Is that the reason why you are treated like slaves in your country?" he further asked. Though I had no answers to these questions, I had begun to boil with anger because the speech struck the right cord in me. I was surprised that a foreign country can tell the story of the Ibos better than the Ibos in Nigeria.

"I want to help liberate the Ibos from marginalization in Nigeria and I want to use you accomplish this task," he said. I have the money to make it happen. I will train you in my militancy group in Libya, give you money and any other assistance needed, and make you a senator in Nigeria. For me to do these, you must do my bidding by converting to Islam. It is my intention to Islamize Nigeria starting from the Eastern part of the country. Once the Igbos are converted to Islam, Nigeria will follow the true religion. For a start, I will give you the sum of $750,000 to enable you undergo three months conversion program to Islam. You will be under the tutelage of Sheik Maliki here in Libya and he will assist you to read and recite the holy Koran. I want you to be a good Muslim that everybody will be proud of in the whole of the Muslim world.

Immediately he was done with his speech, an aide brought a bag filled with money and said, "Your Excellency, this is $1,000,000 for your visitor." "Keep it beside him," replied his Excellency. Chuks sprang on his feet in fear, thinking he was in a trance until his Excellency tapped him on the shoulder saying, "It is real. All these are yours for the mission ahead. He was transfixed on his seat while soliloquizing, "This is an offer too big to be rejected, besides coming from a man whose word is law." Immediately his mind flashed back to Father Albert to confirm the authenticity of what the president told him that many of Nigerian students of the Yoruba, Hausa and Ijaw tribes were getting free education in America. "Why are the Igbos not involved in the scholarship programs? School fees of university students of the Igbos in Nigeria are borne by their families; none by the government. It is obvious that the future is not bright for me in Nigeria," Chuks thought and so decided to take the offer, putting the blame on Nigeria-Biafra war as the main reason for doing so. "I am done with you. Sheik Maliki will take over from here," the President said and took his exit. Chuks was taken to Sheik Maliki's apartment in the magnificent palace and did not see his friends again. With a fat bank account opened for him in Nigeria alongside other motivations, it did not take long time for him to read and write Arabic language as well as recite the holy Koran with much ease.

In Khartoum, Father Albert was visibly agitated as he searched for Chuks all over the place because his colleagues had all returned from Libya. He was reliably informed by his colleagues that he disappeared with Sheik Maliki. Father Albert reported the matter to the police but got no information about Chuks from the police. The government of Libya instructed the powers that be in Sudan to block any investigation concerning his disappearance. Chuks was well tutored by Sheik Maliki in Islamic faith and he became a firebrand Muslim. Basking on the euphoria of his new found love for the Islamic faith, he returned to Sudan, the news spread all over the campus of his conversion to Islam by Sheik Maliki. When the news of Chuks conversion to Islam got to Father Albert, in disbelief he shouted, "This is sacrilegious and the height of apostasy for a boy born and nurtured in the Roman Catholic faith. I should be held responsible for this show of shame because I brought him to Sudan." He sent an official protest letter to the Nigerian Embassy in Khartoum and to the Vatican in Rome but nothing came out of it. The Nigerian Embassy in Khartoum had an all Muslim staff. Besides, the ambassador was aware of whole religious shenanigan that led to his conversion to Islam. For the Vatican, the matter was inconsequential since Chuks was not a priest and not their protégé. Chuks stayed six months in the militancy camp in a remote location in Libya where he was trained in jihad operations. The authority in Tripoli employed Russian snipers who taught him how to shoot AK47 rifles, bomb making, martial arts, and military defense tactics. In the camp he met five Nigerians and others from different African countries. Among the five Nigerians in the resistance camp was Igweniwari, a Muslim from the south-south region of Nigeria. He was to be the anchor man for the jihad in his part of Nigeria. Also in the camp were Shehu and Yusuf of the Kanuri extraction from Borno State. They were training under a false sponsorship of the Kalaria Sect by the powers in Sudan. Chuks became the symbol of the islamization project in Nigeria simply because he was a Christian convert that was snatched from a top priest.

On the day of passing out from the Militancy school, the ruler gave Chuks a Muslim name "Aashif," meaning 'bold and courageous one'. The ruler called a world press conference and introduced "Aashif" to the world as his converted son from Nigeria. Chuks became a beautiful bride courted in the Islamic world. The ruler went on tour of many countries boasting how he converted Chuks into Islam. Back home in Nigeria, the news of Chuks conversion meant nothing especially among the Christian sect because many Muslim faithful had converted to Christianity without any dust being raised. However, it was news among the Mbaise people that he was the first to be converted to Islam in the area.

Father Albert was sent to Rome to work for a couple of years pending the time the negative publicity generated by Chuks' conversion to Islam subsides. Chuks became a super rich, influential and brand name in the Islamic world. The next agenda in the islamization of the South Eastern Nigeria was for him to venture into politics. In this regard, he was sent by the President to an expensive school in Italy to acquire sophisticated political education. In Italy he met Luciano and they became great friends. With the help of Luciano, he opened a charity organization that gave many scholarships – up to university level – to the youths in Eastern Nigeria, sank many boreholes and established schools and mosques. With the help of the authorities in Sudan and Libya, top American and European non-governmental organizations joined them. They rendered free immunization services to children with diseases like polio, measles and chickenpox in Nigeria. Now, nobody talked about his religion but the good work he rendered to the people. Chuks became the man of the people in the Southeast Nigeria and was pressured by his people to join politics because they needed somebody like him to represent them in the Senate, come next election. Chuks foray into politics received the full backing from Libya who mobilized money and other logistics to ensure that the project becomes a reality. For them, this was in consonance with the grand design to Islamize the Igbos in particular, and Nigeria in general.

THE AFTER EFFECTS

FOURTEEN

Paul Bradley was relaxing with his wife, Mary at the prestigious Hollywood hotel suite when the telephone rang. "It is the publisher," said Mary, "he has interesting news for you: a hundred thousand copies of your book have been sold in two weeks." "You still believe James and his lies," replied Paul. "Forget him. Get yourself a drink, sweetie," he said. Immediately, Mary ran toward him in the bathroom saying, "Darling, come and listen to the radio. You are on the news, this is serious!" she shouted in excitement. "Paul Bradley, an American authored a book on the extinct religious group known as the "Kalaria Moslem Sect". The book has generated so much controversy that makes it a must read. The book sold like hot cake in the London international book fair. People believe that the book will break the 200 thousand monthly book sales record held by General De Gaulle about World War II. There have been calls for the book to be translated in other major world languages so that people will understand it well. I wonder what the Muslims will think about it, let's watch and see in days to come. This is Angela Smith, reporting from Washington, for the Voice of America."

"Darling, are we going to pop up champagne in celebration tomorrow, or do we start now?" she asked, beaming with happiness. They were on their honeymoon vacation as a new wedded couple.

"You are on time," said James to Paul as he sat on the chair opposite the couch. "Won't you have a cup of coffee with me?" he asked in a low tone. "No, thanks, Paul replied. James must be up to something Paul thought in his mind. Whenever he is in dire need of something important, he usually speaks in a subtle, low voice. "We need extra fund to successfully execute the publication of this book into six major languages. Our distributors are in need of more copies of your book. Please Paul, you know this is the right time for us to make profits from the sale of the book since the media is awash with the controversy that surrounds this publication that has made it a must read. You are a ruthless businessman always going for the kill when the price is high. Everybody believes your lies without raising an eyebrow. This is a private deal between you and I and the company would not be aware of it," James said to Paul.

FIFTEEN

In the heat of the hot summer afternoon in Tehran the commercial nerve centre of Iran, sat Abdul Khameni on an Arabian carpet, cooling off from the smoke inside a pipe filled with a mixture of brownish desert leaf and dried raw tobacco used by the Arabs as stimulant. He was addicted to a regular smoking of this substance which made him look like a lunatic. His eyes were red like those of a drug addict and he was giving orders to people around him by barking angrily like a drug injected animal. Notwithstanding his condition, Abdul was a man with a split personality, a terror and a hero among his people. He was born in Orabi, a small oasis village near Tehran in the month of August, on the day early seers of the Kalaria sect claims that King Solomon the Israelite married Queen of Sheba against the wish of his people. Till date, it is a commonly held belief by the Israelites that nothing good comes out from the land of Beer-Sheba on that particular day.

Abdul Khameni was born to a poor Kurdish Muslim militant killed in the Kurdish uprising against the Turkish government. He was only eight years old when his father was killed for his involvement in the struggle for the independence of Kurdistan. He suffered untold hardships as a youth because he had nobody to assist him. This forced him to learn life in a hard way. However, Mother Nature smiled on him for he eventually rose from grass to grace through unconventional means to become a hero to some people and enemy to others. He was called the smiling lunatic by his enemies. He was a devout Muslim to the core and observed Islamic teaching and doctrines religiously. At the age of six, he won the coveted prize for Koran recitation held in Saudi Arabia for Muslim faithful globally. He grew up in a harsh neighborhood with the belief that money attracts all the good things of life and without it, one is nobody.

Because of his get rich quick mentality, he dropped out from Islamic primary school and joined the Kurdistan people's liberation front fighting for the freedom of his people from Northern Turkey, against the persuasion of his mother and relatives. He saw the war as a holy one and if he should die in it, he dies an accomplished Muslim. In the army he was the best marksman and was sent to the United Kingdom for series of courses.

However, it was during the war to liberate Kuwait from Iraqi invasion that his combatant skill was tested. At the age of 26, he joined the British army that liberated Kuwait from Iraqi invasion. He developed serious a hatred for the Iraqis because of the untold atrocities committed in Kuwait and for the Shah of Iran for withdrawing Iranian forces from fighting Iraqis in Kuwait on the flimsy excuse that brothers should not fight one another. For him, the Shah of Iran did not give consideration to the massive level of destruction done by Iraqis in Kuwait. When Abdul retired from the military, he settled in Paris and shuttled between Tehran and Paris where he had houses and many wives he frolicked with each time he was in any of these cities. His philanthropic gesture made his people to develop great love for him because of the huge sum of money he donated to uplift them from poverty. Similarly, he was hated by those whom he destroyed their progress in his rise to stardom.

Abdul Khameni became very popular in the Arab world due to his sterling leadership exploits of a very big Muslim sect in Europe and Asia. He was also deeply involved in the struggle for the liberation of the state of Palestine from Israelis' occupation. His charismatic and diplomatic qualities made him a beautiful bride courted by the American Government and major actors in the international diplomatic community. He got a lot of financial favors from the American

Government notwithstanding the fact that they Americans did not like him. He was as wise as a serpent in the international diplomatic circle and especially in his relationship with the Americans. Everything about him was shielded in mystery to many people, especially how he became an instant multi-millionaire. In fact, he was known to tread where angels feared to tread. He wriggled his way out of any situation, no matter how difficult it was. To those who sought his counsel, he always told them that the end justifies the means in the quest for survival.

After reading the publication about the Kalaria sect, his worry now was on how to destroy the book. He called a meeting of the Kalaria sect supreme council on the best way to achieve this and bring to book the lying infidel behind the publication of the book. The means by which to track down the writer of the book was now his biggest concern. To declare fatwa on the book writer or use a hit man to get him out of the way were the options on Abdul Khameni's mind. "Do I declare a fatwa on the book writer? Do we get a hit man from Italy or USA to knock him down so that it will not look suspicious? We have to act fast before this lying infidel destroys our beloved Kalaria sect," he ranted.

SIXTEEN

Senator Chuks was busy in his living room recounting the gains accrued from the illegal oil bunkering deal between him and Mr. Ang. Out of excitement he exclaimed, "Can you imagine this greedy Ang demanding 60 percent of the profit from the deal? I brought the boys that organized and executed it. What a joker he is!" Chuks said to Alberto Luciano, laughing. Alberto Luciano had been his friend since their meeting in Libya. Chuks is now a well-respected and celebrated personality in Eastern Nigeria, having bought his way to the top with funds from Islamist Libya.

Chuks intention to Islamize Nigeria was working according to plan. Being a senator of the Federal Republic of Nigeria, his philanthropic foundation provided free education, built many mosques and few churches. These were deceptive strategies from Islamist Libya. People in the Christian predominant Eastern Nigeria did not mind that a Muslim was behind these. He used one of his wives, a Christian, to get the support of the female folks. He was the national leader of the "Jihad Mafites" even though he used Sheik Atiku as a front. The organization had links in the Middle East and Italy, courtesy of the notorious Luciano's mafia family that controlled most of the crime syndicates in Sicily and Naples. Chuks used his senatorial contacts to transport prostitutes from Nigeria to Italy, sold hard drugs and engaged in illegal oil bunkering.

Chuks succeeds in his criminal activities because the Nigerian Senate was composed mainly of oil bunkerers, advanced fee fraudsters and ex-governors who looted their state treasuries, among others. The Senate allocated millions of dollars to themselves without regard for the plight of the poor citizens. It is on record that the Nigeria Senate is the highest paid in the world. Luciano was marveled with the caliber of politicians in Nigeria which he found unfit to hold political office in the Western world. Luciano teased Alhaji Kamu, a senator from Borno state and close ally of Senator Chuks, "I want to get Nigerian citizenship to enable me become a Senator and have access to wealth in your country. Is there a way you can darken my skin, change my name and get me to the Senate? I hear you Senators earn more than the U.S President."

"That's a lie," snapped senator Chuks. "I have the papers here to corroborate my statement," said Luciano. "You guys make more than 40 million naira monthly from funny allocations to yourselves. That's why your government can not fulfill her civic responsibility to her citizens and your women are into prostitution business in Milan, Italy." "I don't give a damn," said Alhaji Kamu. "My family first and my constituents last. I spent lots of money to win my election. Do you know that I shared rice and meat to thousands of people? Do you know how much I spent to win my party primaries? Party officials collected 5000 US dollars from me at the council level to defeat Mallam Sule. Those guys voted for me because of my money. Even the resident electoral officer in the state was compromised with huge amount of money. You see why a poor man cannot win an election in Nigeria. Anyhow you make your money does not matter to the party and delegates, what they want is somebody that has money to spend. If you emerged as the standard flag bearer from my party's primaries, you will definitely win the election," he boasted. "I need to recover my money first before thinking of the citizens. I am better than the Senators that took bank loan to fund their election." "How can banks fund political activities?" queried Luciano. "That is why I need Nigerian citizenship," Luciano laughed. "Come to think of it Alhaji, how many bills have you sponsored for the eight years you have been in the Nigerian Senate?" Chuks laughed and said that Alhaji only raises his hand to support any bill that will help Senators make more money for themselves. "At least I did not raise my hand in support of the bill making a 15 year old girl eligible for marriage in Nigeria," Alhaji Kamu said.

"Aah we know why you did not vote. Do you want me to tell Luciano the reason behind it?" Chuks responded. "You are free to tell Oyibo Milan," Alhaji Kamu said. "It's not a big deal," he added. Chuks told the story of how a pimp in the senate arranged the services of some pretty Egyptian women in Cairo for five of them – Alhaji Kamu, Alhaji Shehu, Chuks Haifa, Chief Ayodele from Osun State and Alhaji Muktar the Governor of Zamfara State. "We paid $5000 to each of the five beautiful Egyptian girls for the weekend," Chuks narrated. "Were these ladies imported from heaven for such amount of money to be paid to them?" asked Luciano. "Indeed, the girls were truly beautiful to the extent that Alhaji Shehu proposed marrying one of them notwithstanding the fact that she was a minor under the age of 14. He had secretly planned to send his fourth wife away and replace her with the Egyptian girl. We prevailed on him not to do so but he went ahead with the plan and married her after paying $350,000 to the family of the girl. He thereafter sponsored a bill in the senate that would allow Muslims in Nigeria to marry teenage girls up to of puberty as it is done in other Muslim countries. The bill was approved by the majority of the senate votes. Alhaji Kamu did not participate in the voting because he thought he would have been given one of the girls for marriage, without knowing that she was meant for Alhaji Shehu. It is sacrilegious. We have two types of laws in operation in Nigeria one for rich and another for the poor. Just because Alhaji Shehu married a minor, Nigerian marital law had to be changed to allow anybody else to do so. This law was the tonic that these moral bankrupt Muslim Senators needed to bring foreign teenagers as wives," Chuks explained. "These Egyptian girls are firebrand; I feel good each time I have sex with them. Come on guys, have a taste of them; they are a fountain of life," Alhaji Shehu told tell his friends jokingly. Interestingly, Luciano said, "I have a wife and lots of mistresses that I built a Jacuzzi bidet for. When you have an Italian mistress ask her the meaning of Jacuzzi bidet," he laughed.

SEVENTEEN

"It is now my turn to tell you what happened to Senator Chuks in Singapore, the safe haven for his numerous dirty escapades," Alhaji Kamu said. "I was woken up from sleep by the noise that emanated from the show of shame that transpired between Senator Chuks and a transsexual in a hotel room opposite mine during a business trip in Singapore. We were on an inspection tour to buy an oil refinery for refining millions of barrels of crude oil bunkered by General Musa. We fronted for General Musa and other cabals in the Niger Delta region to avoid suspicion by the Niger Delta militants that it was General Musa and not Senator Briggs that owned the oil bunkering ship. There was a disquiet caused by the Northern domination of the oil wells in the region. The restive youths in the region would attack the vessel if they discovered that General Musa, a Northerner, was the owner.

When we got to the Embassy, Chuks spoke rudely to the Embassy staff saying, "Why do you allow these illiterate Igbo traders to import nonsense goods into Nigeria? These traders are the ones responsible for fake and substandard goods have taken over the Nigeria market. I feel ashamed at times to be an Igbo man in the presence of these boys in this Embassy." We had two Igbo boys who assisted us with our shopping in Singapore. I bought a massage bed worth $9,000 demanded by my wife who claimed that the massage bed makes sex very enjoyable. Chuks, always a greedy fellow, bought a lot of stuff loaded inside six big bags which the Embassy guides belabored themselves carrying. As a mark of appreciation, I gave the boys a reasonable amount of money each but Chuks did not. Rather he asked them to organize beautiful women in the night for him. Emeka, one of the boys, organized a pretty girl who happened to be a transsexual, for senator Chuks. I guess it was pay back to Chuks. As the rule of the game, 'money for hand back for ground', we paid $2000 for the night. I saw a transsexual with the semblance of a woman, big breast and seductive voice tone. I did not utter a word because he was not meant for me but for Senator Chuks. Chuks offered the she male an expensive wine to put her in a relaxed mood for the night. When he became tipsy Chuks fully poised for action, started kissing him passionately. Chuks suddenly noticed a rod like object touching his body, instantly he put his hands in that direction and behold a man and not a woman. Chuks shouted, jumped out of the bed like a rat chased by a mean cat. As Chuks put on the light, the she male asked him to come and fuck his anus. Chuks gave him a dirty slap and asked for the refund of his money. The she male screamed on top of his voice which attracted my attention and that of the hotel staff that put a call across to the police. The police immediately raced to the hotel and saw Senator Chuks and the male prostitute with towels wrapped around their waists.

"Haba Senator, this is an embarrassment. Leave the money for him and let us go," I told him. However, he would not listen to me because of his stubbornness. The police wanted to arrest Chuks, but I prevailed on them not to do so because we have diplomatic passports. Immediately I called the Ambassador who instructed his boys to come to the hotel for an emergency briefing. He did not want to be involved in the dirty scandal and therefore directed that the matter be laid to rest. Luciano, if you see Chuks on towel that day, you will laugh to death. He had to let the prostitute go with the money and the case closed. Chuks appealed to the Embassy staff to keep mute over the whole issue and not to let the Press in Nigeria or Singapore to know about it. To this end, we gave $500 to each of the Embassy staff. That is the story of Chuks and a transsexual in Singapore," he laughed, hitting Luciano slightly on the back while saying repeatedly to Senator Chuks, "come and fuck my anus".

"I have a nice write-up on the comparison of education systems of Nigeria, USA and Singapore," Luciano told Alhaji and Chuks. "I want you to read the paper and show it to your friends in the Senate and the Government. Before then, let me tell you a story of what happened to my uncle, Antonio. Don't let anyone know that I leaked this secret to you. You know how agitated Uncle Antonio can be on slight provocation. On one such occasion, he crashed his car in a ghastly accident in Sicily and sustained a deep cut on his lips which was corrected through plastic surgery. He was very skinny to the extent that it was difficult for the surgeon to find a place to cut flesh for the skin grafting. The only place the surgeon found flesh for the skin grafting was on his manhood. The surgeon cut a chunk of skin from Uncle Antonio's manhood and performed a successful surgery on him. However, Uncle Antonio's joy was short-lived, a serious problem set in afterward during sexual intercourse. Anytime Uncle Antonio's manhood got aroused in response to sexual intercourse, his lips would be aroused simultaneously to sex too. His condition was described as unprecedented by experts in the medical world." Everybody laughed after Luciano finished narrating his story. "It is a funny story indeed," Alhaji said.

In his room Chuks read aloud Luciano's book on the relationship between individuals and Government in using education to reduce poverty, considering a comparison of selected sample of First and Third world Nations. It also highlighted the essence of education to poverty stricken people in three selected countries USA, Singapore and Nigeria. "This is interesting," he said and continued reading. "These countries will be broken down into first world, emerging new world and third world countries in the book. It is also of note that some of these countries are multi-racial societies and others with one dominant race will be broken down into tribes or ethnic groups in this paper. The First world countries are Western nations like USA and Germany which are highly industrialized. A classical example of emerging new world country is the little island of Singapore which was termed a Third world country in the sixties but due to a geometric progression of changes it experienced in various spheres of her economy, she has been transformed into a First world nation in a record time of less than 30 years, even without known mineral deposits on her territory. The other classical example is Nigeria in Africa, which cannot be termed a multi-racial country because it is inhabited by 99% people of the black race of different tribes. Race will be divided into tribes or ethnic groups from the same race. This division has affected the country from achieving meaningful progress even though the country is blessed with so much mineral and material resources such as huge deposits of crude oil and a large number of Doctorate degree holders comparable to that of the USA.

In Singapore, there is a multi-racial society composed of about 74.2 percent Chinese, 13.4 per cent Malay, 9.2 percent Indian and others 3.2 percent (Department of Statistics Singapore, 2013). In the USA, the statistics is as follows, 63 percent white, 17 percent Latino, 13 percent black and others 7 percent (US Census Bureau, 2010). In the another study, the Nigerian population figure is doubtful due to double counting that have marred accurate census in the country, given that Federal Government allocates more funds to states with large population figures. Be that as it may, Nigeria is made up of three major tribes of Hausa, Yoruba and Ibo which constitute 60 percent of the total population in such order, Hausa 21 percent, Yoruba 21 percent, Ibo 18 percent and others 40 percent. The country is divided equally into two dominant religious groups, 50 percent Muslim and 50 percent Christian population (National Population Commission of Nigeria, 2013).

Having highlighted the population distribution of these nations, let us examine how poverty level is distributed among various races in these nations in relation to education. From available statistics, notwithstanding the American effort for equal and compulsory education for her citizens, she has not completely eradicated poverty in comparison with Singapore. Although the USA has the best school system and universities among the 50 top ranked universities in the world, in addition to easy access to educational loans like Singapore, it is still not doing better. Based on the above data, one will not be wrong to ask the following questions, "Is there any other thing left undone by the USA? Is the cost of schooling in the USA very exorbitant or is the rating allocated to it wrong?

Let us compare individual and Government effort in providing free and compulsory university education for its citizens. Nigeria is a typical example of a country where the government pays lip service to providing university education for its citizens. Loan or grant facilities are not available for her citizens to further their education to the university level. Although there is free education to an extent at the high school level, the low class families are mostly able to train only the first male child in their families to the university level of education." "Whao! That is the Ibo and Yoruba way; that is not so among the Hausas," he said to himself. He continued to read: "The popular ways many families endeavor to raise money to fund their children's education to the university level is by selling of family land, livestock and treasured possessions, among others. The child is obliged to train another family member in return once he graduates from school and gains employment. Marriage is not immediate for that person until he sends another person to the university." "Not Yoruba people! They would marry immediately!" he winked. "The second person does the same thing and the chain continues like that. In such countries that the presence of government is not felt, it shows that vertical mobility can be achieved by individual effort alone. A lot of people have moved up in societal class and escaped from poverty through individual effort alone. The black race constitutes 99% of the reference group here.

The second case is the USA. There, the government has been striving to eradicate illiteracy and has been providing education up to any level for its citizens through the provision of loan facilities, conducive environment for learning and adequate schools for all. But a lot of people have failed to take advantage of the opportunity, arguing that education is too expensive, no jobs after graduation and that the available jobs are not lucrative enough. These arguments do not hold water enough to some extent because the world is a global village. Education one acquires in the USA is one of the best in the world and can fetch one better paying jobs outside the USA. In this case you can see that the government is making all the effort while the individual is not making enough effort to get educated and move up in the societal class. The multi-racial societies are the reference group here.

The third case is Singapore where government efforts in eradicating illiteracy among her citizens are complemented by individual efforts. These efforts are what the Singapore people are reaping from in terms of having the highest concentration of millionaires in the whole world and a standard of living higher than that of the USA. There is greater individual efforts there than in the USA because the government takes better care of her citizens than the USA government does. Let us see how this has been achieved through education in Singapore. Singapore has only three public universities of international standards but has lots of private schools which are not really of high standards. The government provides loan and grant facilities to her citizenry to advance their education even up to the university level unlike Nigeria which does not make provision of these facilities for her citizens and USA that provides these facilities for her citizens. Having said this, however, the problem with Singapore education system is that it has a limited number of public universities which cannot accommodate everybody. There, the government wants every citizen to get the highest level of education at almost the same cost that US citizens say it is too high and Nigerians will sacrifice anything to acquire it. In addition, the government of Singapore encourages her citizens to apply to foreign universities in case they do not get a space in the public universities in their country. They can school in other countries and get the same quality of education.

With this development, students from Singapore leave their country and comfort zone to acquire quality education to become total persons, thereby achieving the much needed vertical mobility of persons and labor, not only in their society, but also globally. These efforts by individuals and government have made most Singaporeans well educated and it is now termed a society without class or what some people call a 'classless society' because almost everybody operates on the same level of equality. This has thereby reduced undue friction among the different races that make the Singaporean society and poverty is low in the population. The reference population group is multi-racial. However, there is a need for further studies on the link of individual and government efforts in reducing poverty in most societies. The conclusion of this study shows that the combination of individual and government effort will ultimately reduce poverty. Race is not really a determinant of poverty eradication when you compare the differences in US and Nigeria. In the USA the Black Americans have low level of education in comparison to other races there. However, if increased individual effort is put in by the blacks in the USA as it is the case with Nigerians, there will be geometric change in poverty reduction level among the blacks in the USA. Also the belief that in a multi-racial society, dominant race is more educated than the rest is not the case when you compare Singapore and USA. While the minority in USA has low education, the minority in Singapore has almost equal education. This lacuna can be bridged with well thought-out government policies that encourage the minority races in the USA to give more priority to education."

Chuks felt bad after reading the paper because of the scholarship opportunities for the Hausa and Yoruba students only by the Federal Government to study abroad. For him the paper has shown that the Igbo race is the endangered specie in Nigeria because of a war which the government said there was no 'victor, no vanquished'. Does it mean that losing the war amounted to losing their right in the country? He was overtaken with guilt in his mind for compounding their problems the more by making himself a willing tool in the hands of Islamic fundamentalists in Libya, thereby betraying his people, Father Albert and himself. He however consoled himself saying that his action was nothing but a coping strategy of the endangered species – Igbos in the Nigerian society. He believed that the injustice in the Nigerian political system was responsible for his. With such thought, he had no regrets for all he did. Enjoying life to the full is the most fundamental thing now for him and he lay down on his bed and slept off.

Alhaji Kamu laughed sarcastically after reading the paper, saying that education is not for everybody in Nigeria. "It is only for the rich," he said. "If you educate the poor, they will challenge you," he insisted. "Who gives a fuck about how educated Singapore and the US are? They should keep these papers in their country and not corrupt my people," he whined with a curse. "In fact this paper was in effect, operational in the time of Zik, Sardauna and Awolowo not in this modern time he ranted. I will warn Luciano not to bring this inciting junk low profile paper around me again. This paper will generate a lot of public outcry if it leaks to the press and worse of all, it does not add any money to my pocket. Anybody who wants to go to school in my constituency should seek for government scholarship. What do they even need Western education for? Almajiri schooling is good enough for them," he said. "This paper is an incitement against the Northern elites and I will make sure it dies with Luciano and Chuks. The Western nations have no respect for the Third world countries. They say we are corrupt but all the money stolen from our countries are in the western banks!" He was becoming demented the more with anger. "Who is the worse, is it thief or the person that keeps the stolen money for the thief? America, UK, France and the rest are all promoting corruption in my country. That is why Luciano and his likes think we are fools." With that he threw the paper into a trash can.

A Fatwa was placed on the head of Paul Bradley by the Kalaria sect. His execution plan would be supervised by a select Muslim group working in conjunction with the ruler in Libya. The sniper that would take down Paul Bradley would be from a Christian country as that would bring about the least suspicion. The search for the right person for the job went on for a long time without success until Senator Chuks was contacted by the ruler in Libya to look for somebody in West Africa for the job. "It is going to be difficult, but I will do my best," Chuks promised the ruler.

In Rome, Father Albert received a letter from Agidi in Nigeria seeking a favor for his son who wants to migrate to Italy for greener pastures. Agidi was fond of writing letters to Father Albert, but this particular one was different because Agidi raised a lot of weighty issues in it. He passed on information about Chuks and other Biafran children treated at the Red Cross camp in Aba. He told Father Albert that Uzo has become very rich and he is suspected of being a hard drug peddler. Ifeanyi was a scam artist and that the Igbo people were like a leftover food fit only for the dogs. He mentioned that Delta State is bigger in size than Lagos State, Osun State and Ekiti State put together when Anioma

State could have been created to make the South Eastern states 6, like other geopolitical zones. He also said that the seaports in Onne, Calabar and Warri had been conceded and closed down to allow only ports in Lagos to function so that the economy of South East will shut down. Almost all the goods are imported by Ibo's, he noted. For Chuks, he has become a front for Arab Islamic fundamentalist group, the Kalaria sect, which metamorphosed into Boko Haram with the intention of Islamizing Nigeria. He was trained simultaneously in Libya with the Leaders of this Boko Haram sect in Nigeria. Chuks can do anything once money is involved, since he could betray Father Albert who gave him everything when it seemed that all hope was lost for him.

Father Albert read the letter and sat up in his chair, flashed his mind back to the promise of equality, rehabilitation, acceptance and one nation treaty signed between the Nigerian Government and the Biafran forces, which culminated to the end of the civil war. The good boys of yesterday are now the evil men of today. He dropped the letter on the couch with tears rolling down his cheeks and with an angry tone of dejection he declared that another Biafran war was about to begin. This time, it will be between the Crusaders versus the Islamists, he predicted.

EIGHTEEN

Alhaji Kamu completely discomfited his opponent from the anti-corruption party in an election that was marred by violence. He was rigged into office by his people's party which manipulated the ballots collection in his favor. It was a predetermined victory made possible by the resident electoral officer in the state, thereby denying the electorates the right to vote for the candidate of their choice. He is from a Senatorial zone which has the largest population of Hausa Christians in the Chibok area of Borno State where there is so much hatred for Christians in the Local Government Area and who truly never voted for Alhaji Kamu. The election had been won with the help of his Kanuri Muslim brothers in Bama, Banki, Monguno, Ngala, Dikwa and Marte. Shehu of the dreaded Boko Haram Islamic sect was leader of the political thugs that masterminded Alhaji's victory in the polls. Alhaji owes a huge depth of gratitude to Mangu, the Governor of Borno State who introduced him to Shehu Mohammed, the spiritual leader of the sect. The members of the Boko Haram sect disrupted the elections in the Christian dominated areas of the state, thereby leading to the cancellation of the results.

The aftermath of the controversial election in the Chibok Senatorial zone that brought Alhaji Kamu to the Senate drew a lot of political brouhaha from his Chibok community and particularly from Professor

Simeon. He is a social critic and had consistently written articles in the national dailies on sensitive national issues on Confederation, Rotational Presidency, agitation for resource control in the Niger Delta, cessation by Biafra in the Southeast, religious extremism in the Northeast by the Boko Haram sect, election violence and much more. "What is this man up to again?" queried Kamu, in a fit of anger. "This time he is inciting the youths against the political class."

Professor Simeon Wuse's article is a wakeup call for the youths to take their destiny in their hands because they have been deceived by a brigand like Alhaji Kamu and other cronies. The article accused politicians of spending millions of naira in school fees for their children in the best schools in the world. Governor Mangu's children are resident and studying abroad, developing their future and living in affluence. "Politicians are investing massively in their children so that they will continue to rule us after they are gone. They turned you to jobless graduates wearing customized Anti-corruption shirts of the Peoples party, chanting "Change", holding brooms and carrying umbrellas, killing yourself, fomenting troubles and constituting nuisance to the society because of peanuts that can't change your status in society. Be wise and stop being a disgrace to yourself and society for that is the wish of politicians for you. They know if you have sound education and good jobs, they can't use you as political thugs. If Alhaji Kamu and his fellow political urchins cannot bring their children and relatives to the street for campaign, why have you made yourselves willing agents of political violence? In as much as we all want to exercise our political franchise let us not precipitate political war, because if it does occur, it is the poor masses that will bear the brunt. The elites you are fighting for will leave the country for safety with their families in their private jets while you become refugees in other countries if you are lucky to be alive. They will be the same people that will sit at a peace accord meeting in the U.N to decide your fate. They will fly back their families and continue using those who survived the war. Youths listen well. We have only one life to live. What the politicians did in Rwanda is what they are replicating in Nigeria. You and I don't own oil wells and private jets, then, what are we fighting for? They want you to be counted as casualties so that there would be a case for the electoral tribunal. Please say no to violence. If Alhaji Kamu wins, nothing will change because he will not feed his village with his money. We may not live to tell the story if we let them use us again. Be wise this time. Just say "No" to election violence and be "safe". Spread the news! God bless Borno and Nigeria."

Alhaji Kamu was taken aback after reading the article by Professor Simeon. He sighed, saying, "If not for the scholarship that was offered to this stupid Professor by the Islamic bank chaired by me, would he have gone to school? We gave this fool a chance in Borno to get the best of education because he is from the minority Christian extraction in the state, but now he has bitten the very finger that fed him. I will get him," he shouted to himself. "Chibok will never save him, Boko Haram will destroy that infidel and I will have the final laugh as usual," he said. He did not quite understand the type of ideology that Boko Haram was professing, especially the ban on Western education. However, he has won the election and had nothing to do with the brainless Boko Haram boys again. He wanted to discuss with Governor Mangu the possibility of converting Boko Haram boys to a Vigilante group the same way Senator Chuks converted the Bakassi boys to a powerful Vigilante group in the Eastern part of Nigeria. In this way he can use them to hound his political enemies and possibly win the next election. His plans to be a Governor of that state can be given a big boost if he has the Boko Haram boys at his beck and call. He knows top commanders of the sect; having visited Sambisa Forest a couple of times. He was aware that Boko Haram is a tool of the government and can be used to accomplish the Northern agenda of producing a president at all cost. Tuning on to CNN, the news of the overrun of Libya by America and its allies was being discussed. Alhaji Kamu remembered that Senator Chuks and prominent elites in the Middle East had advised the ruler in Libya to move to Zimbabwe where the West cannot touch him but he never listened. As a solution to the ongoing situation in Libya, Alhaji started giving thought to the proposal of Shehu the leader of Boko Haram to help him launder cash and weapons from Libya. Shehu told Alhaji to make a road trip to Mecca and pick up weapons for him while coming back and that Chadian government will give him easy passage because the authority in Libya had already spoken to Chad in this regard. This looks okay to him. However, he did not trust the Boko Haram sect again because of their rapid growth. He was not sure of the relationship between Shehu and the struggling leader of Libya. Alhaji was going to use his intelligence agencies or Senator Chuks who is very close to the Libya ruler to find out if Shehu had real contacts in Libya now.

As a confirmation of Alhaji's fear of Boko Haram, he got a crazy text message from Shehu saying "Master, bills will be signed with bullets and blood. Debates in the Senate and House of Rep will be heard loud and clear with gunshots, and bombs making ratatatatatatata boooooombooom. Motions will be moved in Rambo style, and I assure you that Nigeria will become an Islamic State. Borno State will turn to ashes, if the will of Allah is not allowed to be done. Long live Usman Danfodio! Long live Kanuri! Long live you Senator! He looked at the text message and did not know what to make of it. "Shehu must be crazy," he said. "This guy might be a problem for me, but I still need him," he sighed.

Paul Bradley pondered over his invitation by the United Nations to speak in the six African countries where human rights were stifled by their governments. His wife, however, was particularly interested in Nigeria because of the large population of Christians and in Gambia because of its strict laws against gay marriage which Paul her husband had clearly condemned. He was quite convinced that his book would sell in Nigeria and had already brokered a deal with a local publisher to market his book there. The United Nations was silent over the gay marriage issues but the Nigerian government was very eager to have Paul Bradley speak on the issue while in the country. The government thought of using the opening window to repair its image which has been seriously battered. To that end, it doled out a huge amount of money for public relations. The speech would provide momentary respite for the governments because people would be eager to listen to a Western scholar speak against gay marriage, an issue which had not received the blessing of many western countries. Paul Bradley was only interested in making money. However, it turned out be his greatest undoing.

Unknown to him, a Fatwa had been placed on his him by some top commanders of the Kalaria sect.

Paul's trip to Africa was well publicized particularly in Nigeria because the government had vested interest. Paul would be going to Africa with his wife for the mega talk. It was also a chance for the wife to visit six African countries. She was so thrilled by the fun she was going to catch. The trip was scheduled, hotels booked, venues arranged and it was time to start packing their bags. The main shock, however, would come from his international media conference in Nigeria against gay marriage. The Catholic Church would send a representative too during the media chat.

NINETEEN

In Rome, Father Albert received the news on the capture and death of the ruler of Libya, from Reuter's news bulletin, with mixed feelings. One would have expected him to rejoice over this development given how he turned Chuks against him, but he wished he had repented of his sins and gone to heaven. "Money cannot give you life," he said to himself. He remembered all the visits by the American CIA and Israeli Mossad while investigating the motive for the ruler investing so much in Chuks. The Americans were aware of what Chuks represented in Nigeria and was watching all his moves. He really did not feel a thing but just said, "God's time is the best in whatever one does."

Father Albert was scheduled to address a joint session of the Nigerian legislature during his visit in two weeks time. His speech would center on the need to heal the wounds from series of ethno-religious problems in the country. Also invited for the occasion was a renowned Islamic scholar from Saudi Arabia who is inclined to peace and religious tolerance. This opportunity is very apt, given the high rate of social vices in Nigeria, such as kidnappings in the Niger Delta, killings in the Northeast by Islamic fundamentalists, self determination and agitation in the Southeast, and ritual killings in the Southwest, among others. As a mark of honor for his invaluable contribution to peace in the Southeast, a thanksgiving service and party was slated for him by Biafran survivors in the Red Cross camp at Nkpor. The Nigerian government was also to confer on him a national merit award. This was a ploy to lure him to be part of Paul Bradley media talk which Father Albert would not be interested in, especially considering how controversial the American had become.

Chuks cried profusely when he heard of the disgraceful death of the Libyan ruler. He retired to his private lounge, switched off his phone and restricted himself from any visitor. The whereabouts of the family of the ruler remains uncertain and worrisome to Chuks, although he was not close to his notorious children. When Chuks came to terms with the reality of the death of the Libyan leader, he vowed to avenge his death by killing Paul Bradley even if it involves sacrificing his own life. This has been a standing order given to him by the Libyan leader which Chuks said he could not disobey. The man he trusted to do the job was Shehu the leader of Boko Haram group whom he knew and dinned with at the same table in Libya. Using Bakassi boys to execute this plan will be a direct indictment on him if it is confirmed that they did the job. Another worry for Chuks was that Paul Bradley is an American citizen and as such America would never give up until they avenge his death on whoever that was responsible. Shehu was the man found worthy enough by Chuks to do the dirty job. However, Chuks avoided having any form of contacts with Shehu because of what he turned into. There was rumor that he ate human flesh; while some people claimed that he was a psycho-path with distorted view of Islam that violence is the only way to be a good Muslim. Chuks got a security report from the Islamic Republic of Iran, warning him to stay clear of Shehu. Very soon, with the way things are now, he would become the number one target of the West because he has created an empire of rogues sustained with falsehood, comprised of irate jobless youths without formal education.

The planned assassination of Paul Bradley by Shehu had been concluded. He would be handsomely rewarded and a group in Libya linked to the late ruler would claim responsibility. This decision was taken by top Arab leaders of the Kalaria sect who were very bitter with the Americans for the death of the Libyan leader. "America is nothing but a terrorist nation. How can she make a man, nurture him to stardom, drain his wealth and kill him like a common criminal? Some animals are more equal than others," Abdel Khameni said to Chuks the last time they met. An emissary was sent to Shehu to meet Senator Chuks and Alhaji Kamu at Borno State government lodge in Abuja. Shehu would be airlifted with the Nigerian Army military helicopter to the government lodge, Borno State. He would be protected by Islamic fundamentalists in the Nigerian Army who were sympathetic to the Boko Haram course. Shehu had been able to get away with the heinous crimes against the State because of the support of the Northern dominated army who are mostly Muslims. As a plan to destabilize the Nigerian government, Shehu was to kidnap the Chibok school girls. The girls would be used as ransom to extort millions of dollars from the Nigerian government and also create the impression that the Nigeria government is not capable of handling security challenges. This would make the international community lose faith in the government. This would also provide the North the opportunity they have been looking for to take over power in the country at all cost. They perfected their plans by hiring a top lobby agency in America and a top public relations firm associated with the US government. A Muslim must take over government in Nigeria which is currently occupied by an infidel Christian, come next election. Chuks was never allowed to attend the caucus meeting of the North because he is a Southerner. Even where he was given such access, it was because he was influential in the Muslim world and that he would be useful for actualizing their plans. Chuks was to be used to divide the votes of the Easterners and to whittle down the powers of influential Easterners linked with Israel.

DIRTY DECEITFUL POLITICAL ELITES

TWENTY

Chuks traveled to Abuja on a public transport in order to keep a low profile. He lodged in a roadside hotel using his fake identity and waited for a call from Senator Kamu about the arrival of Shehu to the government lodge. The meeting was scheduled to hold at the dead of the night because of the sensitive issues to be discussed and to avoid being detected by security operatives. Chuks left for the meeting without informing anybody, not even his personal assistant, because he was kept under security surveillance by the Department of State Security Service since the death of the Libyan leader. Getting a phone call from Senator Kamu brought a big relief for him as he was now sure that Shehu made the trip. He drove to Borno State government lodge in a cab and gave the details of his movement to Senator Kamu for easy entrance into the government lodge. While driving down to the lodge, Chuks cast his mind back to the time he was in Libya with Shehu. He recalled a picture of a mean, cold blooded Islamic fanatic with beards like that of a desert fox, observing his prey for every available opportunity. Chuks wondered what in this world made the Libyan leader to surround himself with such hardcore Muslim fanatics. Was it just to Islamize the world? He knew that was a tall dream to accomplish. However, he had no choice but to abide by the rules his master, the ruler had set. He owed a debt of gratitude to him for the enormous power, wealth and fame he has in Africa and the Arabian Peninsula. Even in death, his loyalty to the Libyan leader was uncompromised.

Driving into the government lodge was not that difficult for Chuks because the security apparatus knew of his coming, even though he is an Igbo man, which should have been enough ground to arouse a lot of suspicion at that time. The meeting was an all North affair, except for Chuks who was present because of his strong connection with the powers that be in the Middle East. No one would be expected to enter or leave the building until the erratic Shehu took his exit. For safety reasons, a standby helicopter to evacuate him immediately the meeting was over had been arranged. Shehu was now a beautiful bride to the Northern elites to wrestle power from the South and as such needs to be protected at all cost. Getting to the expensively furnished conference room in the government house was a thing of relief and skepticism for Chuks. It was a thing of relief in the sense that he had finally gotten to the venue of the meeting, and skepticism in that he knew that Shehu can be disrespectful and erratic at times. Seated in the room was Shehu, Alhaji Kamu and Majeed, an Arabian member of the Boko Haram fraternity versed in logistics and bomb making. He was equally a member of a terrorist group in Somali which was responsible for a series of suicide bombing in Kenya and Somalia. He was advocating for the adoption of similar tactics in Nigeria. However, Shehu foot dragged on this strategy because he was uncertain of the gain of using suicide bombers.

Shehu did not extend any compliments to Chuks during the meeting and neither did Mojeed the Arabian, even though they knew one another. To them, Chuks remains an inferior Muslim because he was not of Fulani, Kanuri or Arab stocks, even though they were all Muslims. "What do you want Boko Haram to do for you?" Shehu asked Chuks in the meeting. Chuks told him that he wanted Paul Bradley dead at all cost. This was the wish of the late Libyan leader and must be carried out to the letter. He declared Fatwa on Paul Bradley because the American carried out a lot of blasphemous writings about the Kalaria sect. Paul Bradley would be in Nigeria soon to present a paper for the United Nations and the Nigerian government. In the meeting it was agreed that Shehu will carry out the assassination and that a sum of 5 million dollars would be paid to him through the Central Bank of Nigeria, so that it will not be traceable by any international organization. The Governor of the Central Bank was aware of this and the money would be delivered to Shehu and his men in their bunker inside the forest by an Army General. Another option was to buy weapons of choice for him and to drop them in the forest from parachutes of military helicopters. Shehu and his mate did not alter a word as Chuks made his demand. He sat calmly and stared at Chuks like a wild beast in the Colossa forest. Alhaji Kamu joined his voice, appealing to Shehu to assist Chuks and the Kalaria sect because this is the work of Allah. He spoke in Kanuri language, not minding that Chuks and Majeed the Arabian did not understand the language.

Majeed recorded the proceeding of the meeting with a secret device strapped to the inner part of his left shoulder. This recording will be relayed to the council of elders of Boko Haram for the purpose of extorting money when the time comes. Chuks and Alhaji Kamu were ignorant of the fact that Shehu and his group would use that to blackmail them later.

When Shehu eventually spoke, he said that he was not doing anybody any favor nor was he negotiating with anybody. He told Chuks and the council of elders of the Kalaria sect that Paul Bradley is already a dead man no matter the fortress around him because Allah had never failed him in any fight for what is right. "I will take Paul Bradley down in Abuja in our way without anybody telling us what to do." He then demanded that the 5 million dollars must be delivered within 48 hours. The sect needs the money urgently to recruit more members from Niger, Chad and Cameroon and better equip their cells with much needed precise logistics. He warned that his group would not allow another group to claim responsibility for the death of Paul Bradley whom Allah will deliver to him. With this, America will know that Shehu is not afraid of them, he boasted.

Alhaji Kamu was taken aback by Shehu's threat that he should embark on a lesser Hajj by road so that he can pick up the arms. This did not go down well with him. However, there was nothing he would have done in the present circumstance because if he refuses to do as instructed, the deal would be over and he would face the wrath of the Kalaria sect. Shehu's terms and conditions were agreed without preconditions and Chuks' headache now was how to procure the ammunition from Libya because of the crisis in that country. The next available country to get arms from was the Islamic Republic of Iran with the help of clandestine Hezbollah unit in Nigeria. In this case he would need Abdel Khameni to purchase ammunition from Bosnia or Russia and route it through Kano International airport to Maiduguri and then he would hand them over to Shehu in the forest. Shehu would confirm the receipt of the cash to his proxy in Iran through coded encrypted messages. Talking to Shehu directly at this time was too risky and would rather have to be done by involving multiple links to avoid detection by the Americans. With the Nigerian secret police, he had no fears because of their low professionalism due to corruption. He can maneuver his way easily with them. Chuks paid Shehu cash of $1million in $100 denominations made possible with the help of a Lebanese business mogul, Makram Yousef. He worked for the Iranian secret agency and was a top Hezbollah agent in West Africa in charge of the largest cell in Africa. Makram Yousef had the biggest shopping mall in Abuja and was relied upon to provide cash on short notices in situations like this. His money was paid back with interest even though his businesses were funded by Iran. The Israelis leaked his cover to the Nigerian government but because of the number of jobs he provided, it was impossible to shut him down. Doing so would have made a lot of people jobless. It was a tense situation for the Nigerian government who denied the allegations and exonerated the Lebanese of any infraction by hiring the best lawyers that defended him in court. Moreover, he supported the ruling political party with a million dollar donation during the last election. The matter was closed and Makram Yousef was set free – a decision that did not go down well with the Israeli Embassy in Nigeria.

Shehu did not look like a person living in the forest and waging war against perceived evil men. His smooth texture skin surprised Chuks; it was an evidence of someone living in luxury. His personal lifestyle was a contradiction with what they were propagating. He claimed that western education is bad, yet he fortified himself with sophisticated modern security gadgets and used internet service to send and receive information. He was nothing but a thief and typical Nigerian politician, Chuks thought. "The more you look, the less you see," he reminisced. Notwithstanding falsehood and deception, crazy Shehu would execute the job well as he had never failed whenever it comes to killing infidels.

TWENTY-ONE

Paul Bradley stood in front of a mirror reciting the speech he was to deliver in Nigeria and imagining how Nigerians would react to his speech. "It will be a powerful speech," he said to himself. His support for the Nigerian government against gay marriage would not go down well with the Western press but he was determined to go ahead with the speech because of the big money involved and the opportunity for him to sell his book. For Paul Bradley, the best of his speech would be delivered in the presidential villa in Gambia where the president would be present. His hatred for gays will be exposed more in Gambia.

Father Albert caved in to talk with the Nigerian government while in the country, an idea which he had vehemently rejected because he was convinced that the Nigeria-Biafra war was all about control of oil wealth by Britain, America and French governments. Britain and America supported British Petroleum on the side of Nigerian government while French government supported Elf oil which was on the side of Biafra. These countries had vested interest in exploiting and making oil available to their home countries at the expense of millions of Biafran lives. It was disheartening to observe that western powers, given their interest in the oil wealth in Nigeria, made their cronies leaders and used them to steal oil money while the masses wallowed in abject poverty. The end result is what is happening now – rise of ethnic militias, kidnappings, armed robbery, and cessation agitation by Biafra, among others. Abdel Khameni was convinced that Shehu was certain to succeed in eliminating Paul Bradley because a marabout confirmed it but warned that it would create bigger problems than it was meant to solve. Once this is been achieved, he would call an international press conference condemning Boko Haram. He knew the consequences of killing an American and he had to be very careful with the way he threads on that. Moreover, he was not going to buy arms for Shehu as Chuks Haifa had insisted. Chuks put a phone call across to General Sayeed in Libya instructing him to claim responsibility for the assassination of the American on Nigerian soil as vengeance for the death of the Libyan leader gunned down by the Americans. Chuks lied to him that the hit will be carried out secretly by the Iranians. To further convince General Sayeed, Chuks would release a world conference online from Estonia using a hacker working for the Iranians. He would release fake information from an untraceable internet link just the way he used it in the last election to rubbish his opponent.

Governor Mangu had the hint that the Federal Government had a plan to declare a state of emergency in Borno State because of the activities of Boko Haram. He was shocked at the news because government did not declare any state of emergency when the Niger Delta militants were destroying oil facilities and bombing cities. Why should the North suffer this injustice and his Excellency Governor Mangu disgraced out of office by a Christian and Southerner who the North just allowed to rule? "This will not happen." He swore with his life that it would never happen, rather, this government would be removed at any cost or the North will secede from this country. The news did not go down well in the North and as such, an emergency meeting was summoned in Kebbi town to discuss the issue.

The meeting was well attended by top political elites in the North including those sympathetic to the course of Boko Haram. The meeting was very rowdy; majority of the attendees cast aspersions on the government. They decided that they will use international press to pressure the government to abandon the idea of a state of emergency. After the meeting, Alhaji Kamu and Governor Mangu met the next day in government house and agreed that a good number of girls in Abule Government College will be kidnapped by Boko Haram. This action would embarrass the Federal Government and at the same time put immense pressure on her to abandon the idea of a state of emergency in Borno State.

The principal of Government Girls' college, Abule was summoned to Maiduguri to a meeting with Governor Mangu. She was informed of the intended plan and was threatened with the killing of every member of her family if she did not comply. She was assured that none of the girls will be harmed and would be released after a short period of time. She was told that it was a game plan to return power to the North. She was informed that the girls would be taken from their hostels during their final graduation exams because many of the girls would be present. She would be handsomely rewarded with dollars. In addition, any person she nominates will be made a state commissioner, after the whole incident.

Paul Bradley and his wife arrived Nigeria on board an Arik airways flight from New York to Abuja on a business class ticket paid by the Nigerian government. On arrival at the airport, they were picked up by the protocol officer of the Nigerian Foreign Affairs ministry. They were lodged in Sheraton hotel and towers from where they proceeded on a courtesy visit to the United States Embassy and United Nations Liaison office. The next day they met with senior officials of the United States Embassy before the commencement of the event. Shehu recruited two female suicide bombers and a man to coordinate the detonation of the bombs and take down their prized target, Paul Bradley. The girls were well tutored on how to have access to their target. They were to wear black burqa with bombs strapped inside, carry placards with different inscriptions such as "No to Gay Marriage in Nigeria", "Gay Marriage is Alien to Africa" and, "Do Not Interfere in Our Domestic Affairs". The strategy would make security officials allow the bombers access to everywhere in the conference room. The bombs would be detonated by the man coordinating the operation hidden in the crowd who will put a phone call across to the girls to detonate the bombs.

TWENTY-TWO

The trip of the suicide bombers to Abuja went as planned. They were sheltered for the night in the house of a cell member for the Conference the next day. All the paraphernalia needed for the mission had been procured. It was gathered that the Secret cell member was a top government official. This made it practically impossible for his house to be searched by security officials. He was a mole in the then Federal Executive cabinet but working secretly against the government to wrestle power back to the North at all cost. Mustapha the guide, had plans to have sex with one of the female bomber before they would blow themselves up the next day. It was a ritual among members of Boko Haram sect to sleep with multiple women notwithstanding the strict moral values they claim to uphold.

As promised, Paul Bradley sent a copy of his speech to be delivered at the Conference to the Nigerian government. He planned to use the occasion to address a press conference after his speech on Human Rights Violation and Dictatorship in Africa at the United Nations. The Press conference would condemn gay marriage in strong terms and be a caveat emptor to the Western nations that it will not succeed in Africa, because gay marriage is not in tandem with their culture. They should respect African people and their culture, and stop forcing their outrageous lifestyle on them. Paul Bradley was gorgeously dressed for the occasion. He wore Jack Victor's designers suit and Gucci branded shoe to match. The wife was putting on gorgeous Ichiban dress, nice Prada shoes and beautiful Chinese cut jade jewelries. She was the cynosure of the occasion as all eyes turned to her direction to the extent that many randy men there made passes at her, but she pretended not to notice them.

Meanwhile Chuks and Alhaji Kamu were in Lagos presenting gift items to children in abandoned babies home. They deliberately chose that date as a cover up to what will happen in Abuja and did not want to be anywhere near Abuja. The gift presentation was well publicized in the media because of the caliber of people involved. He told the orphans that he understood their plight because he had similar experience during the Nigeria-Biafra war. He told them that if not for the Red Cross he would not have been what he is today and that their plight now is no limitation to success because there is ability in disability. Chuks sent a text message to Estonia instructing them to get ready to release a press conference once he gives them the go ahead in a couple of hours as the wait continued.

In the deep forest, Shehu was glad that the bunker was complete and the plan to invade Abule the next night was already planned. He would lead this attack with five Generals and fifty foot soldiers. His plan was to haul all the kidnapped girls onto the back of the two open long trailers that was already parked in Abule under the disguise that the trucks broke down and were undergoing repairs. The truck drivers would move into the school once the security officials in the school gate had been overpowered. The plan was simple – bring out all the girls sleeping in the hostel, separate Muslims from Christians and then take all the Christian girls while leaving the Muslim girls. Shehu was also ready to release a world press release through the internet after the hit on Paul Bradley and the kidnap of the girls. He would claim ownership of both acts by describing what the girls wore and would also show some of the kidnapped girls in the video. This video would be in a commando style, depicting him as the new enemy of the west. He would promise hell fire to all non-Muslims and even to big America.

He wants international recognition for his group and the only way of getting it will be to attack American interest.

Mustapha the lead man was in a world of his own in the morning. He was both surprised and excited about the marathon sex he had in the night with the two girls at the same time. "Not even one!" he exclaimed outwardly to himself. This was what the elders of Boko Haram enjoyed all the time – having pretty female sect members whenever they wanted. This is the best sex he had ever had in his life. Wallahi, two beautiful girls at the same time and both girls, beautiful college graduates. He looked at their smooth skin but there was nothing he could do as they were on a good mission for Boko Haram. What he did not know was that one of the girls was an American spy agent, infected with HIV and with an implanted chip in her golden tooth that enabled the American military drone to find out the exact location of the main Boko Haram camp in the deep forest. The Americans were now aware of where the bunker was located, with the help of the spy. They also succeeded in spreading HIV all around the camp as the girl was forcefully passed around the sect's Generals who slept with her without knowing what she was spreading. The damage she did to the sect was great and the only way to cover up was to volunteer for this kind of mission. She knew that the sect would hunt her down and even kill all her family if she was ever discovered to be working for the Americans. Mustapha was now a victim of HIV which he was not aware of at that moment. Paul Bradley and wife arrived the venue of the occasion two hours earlier to make sure that every logistic had been put in place. He was greeted by placard carrying people supporting and condemning gay rights. In the midst of the protesters stood the two girls fully veiled with big placards condemning gay marriage. The girls sat directly opposite each other in the front row so that it will be easy for them take down their target. According to the Somali bomb and explosive expert, people run in the opposite direction once a bomb goes off. The intention of the planners of the assassination of the American was that if he was lucky to escape the first detonation, he will be killed by the second explosion. Cars and vehicles going into the conference venue were checked thoroughly. Men were subjected to serious scrutiny, however, for women the security was a bit relaxed especially for veiled Islamic women as any attempt to search them will generate outcry from Muslims around. The girls were allowed into the conference hall with their bombs strapped firmly on them.

Chuks and Alhaji Kamu waited anxiously to get information regarding the hit operation taking place in Abuja that day from their base at Sheraton Hotel and Towers Lagos. Fifteen minutes into the speech, precisely at the point where Paul Bradley was talking about sit tight leaders in Africa, Mustapha walked outside the building. He put a call to the first girl who detonated the first bomb. The bomb ripped her body to pieces and in the process, killed about fifteen people including Paul Bradley' wife. Survivors scampered to safety in different directions screaming and shouting for their lives. Paul Bradley in an attempt to rescue his wife ran towards where the bomb exploded. The second girl stood up and moved to the exit door. As people rushed towards her direction, she exploded the bomb which killed her instantly and injured Paul Bradley seriously in the process. The total number of recorded deaths from the explosions was thirty five which included foreign diplomats and United Nations workers.

At this point, Mustapha sneaked out of the environment, boarded a bike to the next bus stop to Bauchi. He left immediately before the security operatives began combing the town. He did not wait to confirm Paul Bradley dead before leaving in other to avoid been noticed that he came with the girls. Apart from this he was convinced that the bombs had the capacity to kill anything within 50 meters range and would have killed Paul Bradley. In addition, it was not part of the contractual agreement to confirm the death of Paul Bradley, but to coordinate the execution of the plot. The explosion shook the nation because it was the first suicide bombing that took place in Nigeria. It was a new trend that nobody wanted to hear. Mustapha put a call to Shehu informing him of the success and praising Allah for guidance.

The news of the suicide bombs at the United Nations event shocked the nation and the world at large because it was something unprecedented in Nigeria. It was saddening to the point that Chuks regretted hiring Shehu for the job as he sighted mangled bodies of human beings cut down by the horrible suicide bombs. This was not what he asked Shehu to do. The assignment was to take out Paul Bradley alone but not to kill many people in the process. Although he was disgusted with the carnage, at the same time relieved that Paul Bradley was dead. He went ahead to inform his link in Estonia to release the doctored video claiming responsibility of the assassination from a group in Libya. The video showed the General claiming victory against America and promised more retaliation for the death of the late ruler. The video also warned all Western nationals to beware of Libya and Africa because it will be their waterloo.

Alhaji Kamu was scared of the magnitude of what Shehu did in Abuja and also regretted giving Shehu the go ahead to kidnap girls from Government Girls Secondary School. He planned to have an urgent talk with Governor Mangu the next day to convince him to stop Shehu from kidnapping those girls. From the way Shehu handled the Paul Bradley's deal, he would get in big trouble if he continues to deal with such a raging maniac, sick in the brain.

Abdel Khameni on hearing the massacre in Nigeria called an international press conference condemning the bomb blast in Abuja. He sent his condolence to the families that lost the lives of their beloved ones in the attack. He condemned the use of young Muslim girls in suicide bombings and called it a sacrilege to Islam. He claimed that genuine Muslims would not kill human beings like animals. He claimed that if at all they were Muslims, they were not following the injunctions of the Holy Koran. These were misdirected, confused and bad Muslims, he concluded.

The kidnap of the school girls was easier than expected. There were only two local unarmed security men manning the school gates and they were murdered with ease. The school principal and her family were nowhere to be found, she had relocated her family after she was told of the planned abduction by the Governor. Luckily for Shehu, the senior girls were taking their final English exams and almost all of them were in the school hostel. Three teachers were shot trying to run away. The Vice principal was forced to take Shehu's men to the hostel where all the girls were separated in groups of Muslims and Christians as planned. More than two hundred Christian girls were marched into two trailers and the remaining ones joined Shehu's men in the small trucks. Shehu now had his price and the decision of what to do with the girls would be taken by the council of elders of Boko Haram and not those lousy politicians. This was probably the best attack he had done, as he lost none of his men in the attack and everything went according to the plans.

Paul Bradley was badly injured from the bomb explosions. His left leg was shattered and in the process, he lost a lot of blood. He was given 10 pints of blood in the intensive care unit before he was flown to New York in an air ambulance. His recovery process was kept a top secret by the American officials because they were afraid that the assassins were still after him and they had to find out the motive for the attack.

In Libya General Sayeed saw a video showing him claiming responsibility of the Abuja attack and was shocked at what Chuks has done. He quickly released a press conference denying any knowledge of the attack in Nigeria, even though he expressed happiness for the dead American in retaliation for his dead boss. He was was not happy with Chuks and vowed to pay him back one day. Meanwhile, security agencies had placed a huge reward on any information that will lead to the arrest of the planners of Abuja attack. Video replays did not reveal anything to the security agencies, so the Americans were invited for proper forensic examination. The problem, however, were the conflicting reports emanating from Libya about the attack, with one group claiming responsibility and the same group denying it.

The news of more than 200 Christian girls kidnapped from the Abule School shook the nation's airwaves. Shehu split the kidnapped girls into four groups and sent each group to a different destination, having sensed that there would be a massive search for them by security operatives. Some were sent to Cameroon, Chad, Niger and Mali. He was happy that his action had drawn global attention and in a matter of days he would be taken seriously onward. Many Western nations placed a security alert to their citizens traveling to Nigeria. This news made Alhaji Kamu jittery because Shehu had out maneuvered him this time. He was scared of what would happen to the girls and there was nothing he could do now even though he was in Maiduguri to see

Governor Mangu. He had to rush down with Governor Mangu to assess the situation of events in the community which had been thrown into mourning. Almost every family was affected by the abduction. Professor Simeon Wuse wept profusely because two of his daughters were missing.

Father Albert was afraid of his safety when he heard of the bombings in Abuja but when he remembered the difficult times of the Biafra war he was encouraged to embark on the trip to Nigeria. "I must go to Nigeria and address the Senate even if another terror attack is going to happen. I am an old man getting close to my grave, so why should I be afraid of death?" he said to himself. Shehu posted a video on YouTube showing some of the captured girls weeping beside him. He claimed responsibility for the kidnap and suicide bomb attack in Abuja. He threatened to sell the girls out as slaves if America or the Nigerian government tried any rescue attempt. He warned America that their plan to gas Sambisa camp and rescue the girls was well known to them. He showed the world his gas mask and said Allah reveals everything to his children through friends in high places. He thanked Allah for letting them kidnap only Christian girls and that they would be converted to Islam by force.

TWENTY-THREE

Lots of resentment greeted Shehu's action following the kidnapping of the harmless school girls. This was especially from the Islamic world which claimed that the act was anti-Islamic and a shame to the Muslim world. Abdel Khameni called him an evil Muslim of the dark ages while the international community described him a paranoid jihadist. But in all this, some groups supported him and this drew lots of followers to Boko Haram. Basking on the euphoria of his successful kidnapping of the girls, Shehu went berserk and started robbing banks, raiding villages for food, raping and killing anyone that was sighted.

Father Albert had made up his mind to go to Nigeria especially as he had been given enough assurance by the Nigerian government of maximum security on arrival. This was against the appeal from the Italian Embassy warning him against traveling to Nigeria at this time. People in Nkpor pleaded with him to make the trip as this might be the last time they would see him before he goes to his maker because he was older and looking very frail. Father Albert got to the Lagos international airport enroute Abuja for the first time in twenty years and to his surprise it was in a worse condition than the last time he visited it. The air cooling system was not working and the elevators were in terrible conditions. "Is this not a shame to call such an eyesore an international airport? How come a country with the highest number of private jet owners in Africa and huge revenue from oil sales cannot maintain such an important edifice and gateway to the outside world?" he thought. At the immigration checkpoint, Father Albert was asked to bribe his way into the country by officers of the Nigerian immigration service. "What is going on now in Nigeria?" he asked the officer in annoyance. Before the Nigeria-Biafra war, the country was a model to others, now it looks like a ghetto. He was indeed pissed off and did not know when he let out his venom on the officers.

It was a warm welcome for Father Albert by the Nkpor community officials and representatives of the Nigerian government before he was driven off to catch a flight to Abuja. While in the cab, he told the driver to slow down to enable him have better view of the environment. It looked worse than the periods before the war. Driving in the crazy Lagos traffic jam was like hell and kill joy to him. It took almost two hours to get to the local airport that normally should be a fifteen minutes journey. The roads were bumpy and untarred. He was really disappointed with the level of decay that he saw in Lagos. This is a disaster that the Senate needs to be told without bulging. Getting to the local airport, it was not different from the mess he had witnessed earlier. As he got to the airport, an airport scam artiste approached him and told him that he could bypass without paying the airport duties if he registers in their stand. His driver quickly sent the scammer away, warning Father Albert to be weary of his luggage else, this guy would disappear with them. Father Albert was furious and asked an airport official why they would not arrest the man and to his surprise, he was told by the airport official that it was none of his business. "Is this how Nigeria now works?" he asked in disbelief. "There is no law and order again. The decay is very deep," he noted.

On arrival at the Abuja international airport, Father Albert was driven to Nicon Noga Hilton hotel by a government official. He was unimpressed with the expensive nature of his hotel suite. He insisted on leaving the hotel for a cheaper one the next day. It was not in his calling to live that kind of luxurious life when there are many people in need of help from the government. The government officials moved him to a cheaper hotel according to his wish.

Notwithstanding the assassination attempt on Paul Bradley and the kidnapping of the school girls, the Senate leadership insisted that the anniversary celebration would go ahead as planned. They wanted to tell the world that Boko Haram cannot stop the country from moving forward. The arrival of Father Albert and the Imam from Saudi Arabia for the occasion boosted their confidence the more. The news of the survival of Paul Bradley was a huge shock to Abdel Khameni. He got up from his chair after answering the confirmation telephone call, pranced around the room, looked up to high heavens and sulked back to his cozy chair. He knew that nobody will ever get Paul Bradley again in life because America would ensure that he is protected for life. He was scared that Boko Haram might expose him as the mastermind of the attack after he criticized them.

Chuks Haifa was disappointed with Abdel Khameni because he had failed in his contractual assignment and he therefore avoided picking his calls. "I don't know how I can explain to the Kalaria council of elders that I knew nothing about the failed attempt on Paul Bradley. Why this mistake and why using Boko Haram when other people could have done the job neatly without raising all this publicity in taking down a single individual," Abdel thought deeply. The mistake had been made and they had to live with it. He was now in a dilemma as to whether to send condolences to the American government on the attack on Paul Bradley as a diversionary measure but he was not sure how his group would take it. This step, if taken wrongly, might result in his death. He was now in between the devil and deep blue sea, as only intelligence and luck will play out for him now.

Agidi accompanied father Albert to Abuja for the occasion and they stayed in the same hotel suite, recounting the good old moments. Agidi narrated to him how the Easterners have been neglected since the end of the war and how this had given rise to the agitation of new Biafra by a group of young men who did not witness the horrors of the Nigeria-Biafra war. The people are demanding that the government provide the region with basic infrastructures such as good road, electricity, access to good education and jobs, among others. All these agitations would fizzle out once they are met. He laid the blame on the doorstep of the politicians, invoking the wrath of God on them and their families.

Chuks Haifa never wanted to take part in the event because of the fear of what Father Albert might say about him. He suspected that his political enemies instigated the invitation of Father Albert to speak to the Senate. He discussed it among his friends in the Senate who insisted that he attends the occasion and put his enemies to shame. But they warned him to keep a low profile throughout that day as he had no other business with Father Albert again. The Senate building was beautiful to behold, it was designed like an exotic mosque with the interiors expensively furnished. Father Albert was ushered into the occasion and sat beside the Imam from Saudi Arabia. Imam Mansur's speech was wonderful and well applauded because his speech linked religion to most of the problems in the society. He mentioned that a strengthened love for all religion would make the world a better place. Most of the time, religion is where you were born into and all religion should be respected. He talked of love and the need for all to live together in peace.

Father Albert sighted Chuks sitting at the far end of the building. He wanted to go and confront him but because he had little time to make his speech, he had a change of mind. He was introduced by the Senate President as a true son of Nigeria, who helped the poor and needy during the Biafra war. He was referred to as 'Father Red Cross' and there was an outburst of emotions as people kept standing up and clapping for him while the introduction was going on. In his opening speech, he thanked Imam Mansur for a wonderful speech delivered. "I am Father Albert; I know most of you do not know me very well. My mother was born a Bosnian Muslim and my father a German Jew. I am the only child of that union and I am a Catholic Priest today. In my DNA result that I got some months ago, it was revealed that I have 5% African gene, 6% Arabian gene and the rest European gene. Then how do I describe myself now? Am I not one in all?" He raised his voice and his two hands and looked around the room in a menacing manner. "The same applies to all of you here. If you are in doubt, go and check your DNA gene, I am pretty sure that there will be a little Hausa, Yoruba, Igbo, Ijaw, Efiok, Uhrobo, Fulani and Tiv gene in each and every one of you here. Then why do you hate one another? You are deceived by different religions, tribes and languages to work against each other in this your country. The divide and rule system introduced by your colonial masters still deceive you up till today. Looking around, I see hatred for each other in the eyes of everybody here. You fought a war because of this and you are moving towards another war. Can't you learn some lessons? I speak as a witness of the last war and also an elder who is supporting nobody. I have no financial interest at all but speak the truth. The civil war ended with the slogan 'No Victor, No Vanquished,' so why should the Igbos agitate again for a new Biafra if they were fully integrated and taken care of? You members of the Senate and House of Representatives," pointing his right fingers round, "are part of the problems. Walking into this compound, I have seen the type of cars that the Prince of England does not drive. I smell so much affluence right here but I smelt poverty outside. I do not see men with conscience here. What I see is a group of people that corner all the wealth of the nation.

You do not care at all. It is now a matter of 'me and my family'; the rest of the people can go and die. You allocate all the money to yourselves and leave nothing for the masses. It shall come back to haunt you very soon if you do not follow the way of the righteous. The land is not for the few but for the people. A lot of you here that participated in winning the war shared the spoils of the war amongst yourselves, allocating oil wells and stealing from the people. The wicked shall die one day, he said. Nobody is buried with all his money. Let this money trickle down to the masses. Enough is enough!" he shouted. "God is watching and he watches every day," he said. "We have to forgive and that is what I expect all of you to do. I will show the world that forgiveness comes from God and man at the same time." At that point, he called Senator Chuks Haifa to come up the podium and join him. This was a shock to Chuks, for he never expected this kind of thing to happen. His mind ran the race of its life. "What is this man going to say?" he wondered. At that point, he regretted coming to the event. He prayed that the ground should open up and cover him. Father Albert had to repeat it that he wants his long lost son Senator Chuks to come and join him on the podium. At that point the political enemies of Chuks starting shouting and urging him to go to Father Red Cross. They were anticipating a disgraceful lambasting of Chuks from Father Albert on the podium. Alhaji Kamu at that point tapped Chuks on the shoulder and told him to go and see the elder pastor. Chuks stood up like a man in trance, how he walked up to the podium, he could not remember but the next thing, he was up there with Father Albert. Father Albert looked at him closely for the first time in a long time and proclaimed, "I want my son back." He said, "I have forgiven you a long time ago for what you did to me. He drew Chuks closer and hugged him with tears trickling down the eyes of both men. Everybody in the building stood up and applauded, except the political enemies of Chuks who were not impressed by this silly show of Father Albert. Father Albert now directed Chuks to stand beside him till the end of his talk and continued by urging everybody to forgive and live together as one in Nigeria. He ended his speech reminding the lawmakers that it is time the 'scars of war are borne by the dead and not the children of the defeated'. "Long live Nigeria!" he shouted a couple of times more. As he stepped down the podium, everybody stood and applauded this great adopted son of Nigeria, Father A Albert.

ABOUT THE AUTHOR

Obi Nnanna Nwabugwu, a Nigerian-American, lives in Oklahoma City, Oklahoma. He started from ADJS, Mbieri. He holds a bachelor's degree in Insurance from the Imo State University, Owerri, Nigeria. He has a Diploma in Information Technology from Knowledge Windows Asia Pacific Institute, Singapore. He had Nursing training at Concorde Career College Grand Prairie, Texas, and has a Masters's degree in Human Relations with a Concentration in Clinical Mental Health Counseling at the University of Oklahoma. He worked with the Nigeria High Commission, Singapore; TMG Servicing; Fireman's Fund Insurance Company, Dallas, Texas, Shadow Mountain Behavioral Health, Tulsa, Oklahoma which is a member of the UHS group, Military Family Life Counselor, Camp Butler, Okinawa Japan. A director with Ndiigboworlwide.com, Ikukuomafoundation Nigeria, and 12-step Addiction Rehabilitation Ltd Owerri Nigeria. He is presently a Mental Health Counselor with NewLife Youth and Family Counseling Services in Oklahoma City. He is not a career writer but writes fictional books for fun to highlight pressing issues in the society.

www.ingramcontent.com/pod-product-compliance
Lightning Source LLC
Chambersburg PA
CBHW021738190726
48288CB00009B/3093